A Twisted Tale

Story Of Manipal

Anand Kumar

Invincible Publishers

First published in India in 2017 by Invincible Publishers

ISBN: 978-93-86148-65-0

Invincible Publishers

G - 120, Sushant Lok III, Sector 57, Gurgaon-122002

Opposite Kasturba Ashram, Radaur Distt Yamuna Nagar, Haryana- 135133
Digitally Printed at Replika Press Pvt. Ltd.

Dedicated
to all those
who have
loved and lost!

Acknowledgment

* * *

I have always dreamt of this day! When I would get to write an acknowledgment and thank a hell lot of guys and gals with some fantastic words. But finally when this opportunity has turned up, I feel short of words. It may sound strange that an author is short of words but that's what my condition is!

There are so many things in my mind, I don't know what to put down in black and white and what not. There is a saying in Hindi, "*Akela Chanaa Bhaad nahi Phorta*" and that's what I genuinely feel about this novel. I won't dare say that it's my work alone. No way! If you are holding this novel in your hands, it's because of the collective efforts of many.

First and foremost, I would like to thank my close friend from B.Pharm, Ajit Vikram, who we lovingly call Vicky. He was my roommate for four years and there was never a dull moment with him. It's only because of his constant motivation that I sat down to write this novel. Regular reminders and follow ups from this guy made a lazy guy like me finally finish writing this novel. I owe a lot to you.

Manisha Chhabra, the constant chatter box, my friend from M.Pharma, who has more faith in me than I do myself. She was entirely sure that I could accomplish writing this novel, despite the serious doubts that I had in myself. She was completely involved in the process, right from the initial conceptualisation of the story to the sequencing of chapters and reading drafts after drafts to check for errors. Ever since I have met her, she has been a strong pillar of support in my life.

I can never forget the contribution of my other Manipal friends and seniors! Each one of them is very special and so close to my heart. Some of the characters in this novel are inspired by real people from my own Manipal experience. They have made me a better person and my life happier. I am really thankful to Aditya Ranjan, who is the "*Haldhar Bhaiya*" of my life. Please continue to be so! Shelly Garg, who taught me the virtue of being calm and smile through all odds; Adya Saran, who has the innocence of a child and the might of a bull, a deadly combo indeed! Anshuk, always the victim of our pranks, thanks for bearing with me; Suryakant, who taught me how to tackle pain and loss in life without useless rumination over it; Arvind Mohan Upadhyay, our very own AMU, who taught me that hard work is always the key and that there is no shortcut to success. Dinesh and Diksha need a special mention, as they were my lab mates and were really patient in making me understand the practical sessions.

I was very lucky to get the guidance, love and affection of my seniors. Surojit da will always remain a respected person in my life. It was him who made me realize that I could be successful in the creative field. Special thanks also to Deepa Rao, who was an integral part of our creative team and whose smile was as good as Madhuri Dixit's, if not more.

My juniors: Rahul, Avilaw, Zaki, Shashank, Dhananjay and many more who made my Manipal life great! I owe a lot to my lecturers and professors and I am indebted to each and every one of them, especially Uddupa Sir, Manthan Sir, Shreedhar Sir and Mallik Sir. To make idiots like me study, is never an easy job.

I am thankful and grateful to this place Manipal, where I came as an ignorant young lad and transformed into a mature sensible man, with a better understanding of life. Thanks Manipal for making each and every day of my stay here so memorable.

The list will be incomplete without the mention of my childhood friends Amit, Prashant and Praveen. Our friendship had seen more than thirty years and it's a blast whenever we are together.

I am really thankful to Anuja Ahire, the sweet and cute girl who came with an oasis of love to my deserted life when I needed it the most. She is now my better half. The kind of patience and understanding she has shown is impeccable.

If there is one person who has been the strongest pillar of support in my life, it's my mother. The person that I am today, is all because of her. She is the best mother of the world! My dad is a man of very few words but his love for me makes me wonder how lucky I am!

I am also grateful to my *Dida* and *Dadu* who pampered me a lot all throughout my childhood. I miss them a lot.

Most importantly, I would like to thank my publisher, especially Mr. Ajay Setia, for showing faith in a first-time writer.

My acknowledgment would not be complete if I don't mention the name of Chetan Bhagat. He has been my inspiration and my guru ever since I read 'Five Point Someone'. I have learned a lot from him. He is just like "*Guru Dronacharya*" for me and I am his "*Eklavya*".

June 2005, 11 AM, MCOPS, Manipal

* * *

It was my first day of M.Pharm. I wasn't too excited as I had completed my B.Pharm from the same college, i.e. "Manipal College of Pharmaceutical Sciences". Everything was same for me - same college, same labs, same library, same playgrounds, same teachers, and the same canteen. In fact, I was a bit sad and gloomy as none of my close friends were pursuing M.Pharm from here. I was left alone in this place,'Manipal' for two more years to complete my PG. It was my second orientation program in this college. I had already attended one in B.Pharm. I always had a strong disliking for all such academic rigmarole where these self-styled erudite and experienced professors lectured us about our futures, goals, and motives in life. But I did not want to end up on their 'hit list' on the very first day by bunking the orientation. Moreover, it was at 11 am, so I didn't need to get up early and could also check out the new chicks. New chicks are always a centre of attraction for any guy in Manipal, so I decided to give it a try. The orientation was going on smoothly. A few senior professors delivered some crap in the form of their introductory speech. Some of them even tried to crack jokes. Hardly did anyone laugh at their jokes, which were an absolute insult to the word joke itself. Those were the same boring jokes, which I had been hearing for the last four years. At last my Principal, whom we fondly call *Princi* reached up to the mike. The way he held the mike reminded me of Russell Crowe holding his sword in the movie Gladiator. He had a unique style of speaking. Whenever he spoke, he would look up as if speaking to a ceiling fan. Yes, I was accustomed to that idiosyncrasy of his, but for the new students it was more of a shock. Some gutsy guys even had a squat laugh. His way of speaking was more like humming of a bee. I was not at all interested in his speech and was kind of dozing when I heard my name. My dear Princi was saying, "We are very strict about attendance. If you are short even by one percent you will not be allowed to appear for the exams. Then you should not come to me. That's why I gave you Akash's example. He had shortage of attendance in 6 subjects during his final year and had to write assignments day and night to make up for his attendance. If you want to know how strict we are, you can ask Akash as he has faced these situations personally. I expect you to improve this time Akash."

Improve! My foot. Can somebody please tell him that perfection can't be improved? Well, that's what I used to think about myself – 'I am perfect!'.Moreover, no one there was interested in his crap. He still continued, "So can I expect a better commitment this time from your side, Akash now that you are in PG?"

What is wrong with him? Has he forgotten that he is in the middle of an orientation speech and its not an one-on-one conversation with me? That's the problem with these scientist type guys. They can do all sorts of absurd things possible under the sun. What does he expect me to do now? Stand up and give him a nod confirming my commitment? This is never going to happen anyway. Until now none in the auditorium knew who this 'Akash' was and to whom was he speaking. Thanks to the way my Princi looked up at the ceiling fan during his lectures and speeches. But now, I had to reply. I stood up and with a nod of head, I gestured my commitment. Alas! All eyes were glued on me. They were trying to figure out that how the master bunker, stupidest of all, most careless and idiot guy looks like! I wish I had not attended this orientation. It was extremely embarrassing and humiliating. What an impeccable introduction it was with my new batchmates!

After the orientation got over, there was a customary tour of college to acquaint the new students with the campus. During that tour, I was the centre of attraction. Everyone had an opinion about me and of course, they had comments too. Nishtha said, "Akash, there are only seven subjects in the final year, and you had shortage of attendance in six. You must be a really lazy guy."

'Yes, you fat lady I am lazy.

But it doesn't seem that you work out much. You are like a balloon ready to burst. Why don't you do something about your *Golgappa-* like cheeks than thinking about my laziness?' But humbly I just said, "Well I could have a shortage in all seven. But I managed to be regular in at least one subject. See I am not that lazy." Even the studious and serious looking guy called Saikat got a reason to smile. A few minutes later, I again heard Nishtha saying to Khan, "These are the kind of guys who spoil the name of great institutes like Manipal. No wonder he could not clear entrance of any other college and is here only because of an internal quota." I ignored. I could have easily replied that Manipal was the only entrance I appeared for and I got admission through general quota and not internal quota. I still chose to ignore. The only thing I learnt during my Bachelor of Pharmacy was to ignore. That's how my first day of Master of Pharmacy pictured out!

College Days

* * *

On the second day, after the lectures were over, I was sitting in the hostel canteen sipping my evening tea with my Wills Navy Cut. Kislay joined me. Kislay was my batchmate in B.Pharm and like me he too was also continuing his M.Pharm here. Kislay is a baby faced, sweet looking adorable kind of a guy, good at heart who could never harm anyone. Although we had been in the same hostel for four years, we were not very good friends. We were more than the superficial 'Hi Hello' kind of friends, but not very close. He had his own group and I had mine. Now that just the two of us were left from B.Pharm days, so out of familiarity, we usually spent time together. At least I knew him, unlike my new batchmates whom I had never seen before.

"Hey Akash, how is it going?"

"Cool"

"What *yar,* you bunked the last lecture? Any engagements?"

"*Na yar*. Just got bored. You know I can't handle too much of lectures. It's bad for my health.," I said refreshing his memory of my attendance stories. I was in the same ignorant mood as always.

"Ha ha ha. You try to be better this time around dear. PG is not as easy as UG."

I let those remarks go by, as I was not sure if that was just a passing comment or a genuine concern for me. It was better to enjoy a ciggie and tea, than dissecting and analysing his statement.

"So Kislay, how do you find our new batch? Anything interesting?" I just asked for the sake of conversation.

"*Yar*... there is this one girl, who seems really nice. She is very friendly also. I went out with her for coffee," Kislay told with a broad smile.

"Nice progress dude. Coffee on just second day. You seem to be moving very fast. Great!"

"Nothing great *yar*. We paid in American Style." American Style payment means GTPS (Go Together, Pay Separately) i.e. although we go out together, we pay our own bills. No one bears the other's expense. This is usually followed during booze sessions at Downtown or Jewel Rock. The guys who drink less always fear that they might have to pay more if the whole bill is equally divided. So better keep a track of your number of pegs and pay accordingly. However, when we go out with girls, this system changes dramatically and we are back to the Indian style, where we always feel that the males should pay the bills. Paying the bill for a girl is the first step of becoming her boyfriend... oops,

Body-friend in Manipal. No doubt Kislay was upset. "You did not insist on paying the bill?" was my query.

"I tried but she denied. She told, we should split the bill if we want our friendship to last, so I just kept quiet."

"Hmmm..." I threw my cigarette butt away. Kislay

was expecting some kind of reply but my reaction was too dull.

"What? Tricky situation, right?" Kislay was pushing me to say something.

"You could have said that Manipal is like your second home as you have stayed here for four years and now that she is at your home, it's your duty to take care of her at least for first few days, which of course includes taking care of her food and when you will be at her home town she can feed you as much as she likes and you will never stop her. In this way you could have indirectly self-invited yourself to her home town."

"Wow dude! you very well know how to play with words. I could have never thought of these things. Only a director can think like this. From today you guide me how to tackle that girl. You are really a Love *Guru*."

Love *guru*...Oh no, again that word. I got this tag of Love *guru* in my second year of B. Pharm. I don't know why and how my friends started calling me by that name. May be it was because I always had a lot to say whenever it was a matter of love or may be my suggestions were effective. May be because I had conveniently helped many guys to catch hold of their respective girls and most of them became successful pairs. May be because I used to write romantic Hindi poems and I was very emotional. May be because I was in love with a girl who was one year senior to me and everyone believed that she was a very hard nut to crack and that she was never going to reciprocate my love.

"What are you thinking *yar*? Tea is finished. Shall we go to the End Point?" Kislay disrupted my chain of thoughts.

"End Point is a good option. There is nothing to do as such. Let's go."

End Point is really the end point of Manipal.

Manipal actually is a kind of small valley which ends at a point. One can see the river flowing down at the footstep of the hill. You are mesmerised by the beautiful scenery at evening with sun setting down at the far away hill, river flowing down and big trees around. It's the favourite place of the couples. Nice place to date in the lap of nature or in the lap of your beloved, whatever the case may be. For guys like us 'End Point means the point where we booze all night' under the dark sky in the cover of stars with cool breeze coming from Arabian Sea and listening to the musical wave of flowing Suvarna River. We had celebrated many birthday parties at the End Point, drinking and dancing all night. No wonder I had attendance shortage in six subjects in final year and my dear Princi continues to curse me until this date. We walked through LH (Ladies Hostel), CL (Central Library), and our college MCOPS on the way to End Point.

"Akash I have come to End Point so many times but every time it feels new. The cloud, the trees, the breeze, the grasses, and the rocks they look different every time. Don't you think so?" Kislay's internal poet was surfacing out. It is better to leave a person alone or at least let him feel alone when he is in such kind of a mood. Almost every second guy of Manipal has come on a date at least once at the End Point. This explains the reason for Kislay feeling poetic. May be some of his old sweet memories were hidden there. We were not close enough during UG days to know about his personal life.

I was uncharacteristically quiet. Kislay must have noticed that.

"Akash *yar*, you are very quiet. It seems you have some old sweet memories associated with this place. Isn't it?"

Oh my God. Kislay is thinking the same thing

about me what I was thinking about him. Do we guys think anything else other than girls or things associated with girls?

I was in dilemma what to answer. Shall I tell him the truth? The truth which was known only to a very few close friends of B.Pharm. Should I share my past life with him? There seems to be no harm in that. But I had never spoken about that to anyone.

"Hey Akash, tell *yar*. We all knew that you had some kind of an affair with that Neelu Shenoy, our senior. Did you come on a date with her here?" Kislay's look was nothing more than inquisitive. All guys are bothered about other's affair.

"It's a long story buddy. Let's keep it for some other day."

"We have a lot of time *yar*. Its only 7 pm and hostel gate closes at 12 midnight." Kislay was in no mood to let that opportunity slip away. After all, he was about to peep into the Love *Guru*'s past. All my batchmates wanted to know that how I managed to date Neelu Shenoy. Neelu Shenoy, girl with a killing smile, silky voice, pleasing, charming personality and a down to earth nature. She had a divine innocence on her face and possessed beauty with simplicity. She always reminded me of Waheeda Rahman. She was crowned 'Miss Valentine' for three consecutive years, also a very good singer, and dancer and let me not forget to mention, obviously an actor too. Even the topper of their batch could not manage to date Neelu. As a matter of fact, many of the engineering guys from MIT also tried, but all in vain. So it was a kind of mystery to everyone that how she finally fell for me, a guy, who is nothing more than average in looks, studies and even bank balance.

"You really want to know ...Kislay?" I was rather questioning myself, whether I really want to tell.

"I can't wait. Is it Neelu, who you took out on dates here?" We comfortably sat on a rock. I lit my ciggie. With the first puff ...I started speaking.

First Date of Manipal

* * *

"I met her many times here. But I can never forget my first date here."

"What was so special about that? Did you kiss her?" Kislay was jumping to conclusions on his own.

"No *yar*, there was nothing that great in that date. I remember it because she was not ready to come to the 'End Point' and..." Kislay interrupted me.

"Being spotted at the End Point meant that it became official and that you are involved with that guy. No doubt she was not willing to come. After all she was not like other chicks. So how you managed *yar*?"

"I had to fast" was my short reply.

"Fast? Means you left eating? How? I mean what you exactly did?" I took a long puff.

"I still remember. It was in second year. We were talking outside LH at about 6 pm. We both were hungry. I asked her to come to Shack Point for some snacks."

"Isn't Shack Point in the End Point itself? So you were indirectly asking her to come to End point."

"Yup Kislay. You can say so."

"Oh and then what? Did she deny straight away?" Kislay was looking very eager. "No, she did not deny right away. But she had lots of excuses for not coming..."I took one more puff of ciggie.

"Excuses like..."

"All bull shit pretext like it's getting late and she has to study, she needs to be in her room as her parents could call anytime on her landline number, her roommate was not well and she has to take care of her." Kislay could not digest it, "That's crap, absolute crap. She was talking to you outside LH and she was not going to be in room anyhow."

"I knew it was all crap. That's why I kept pushing her to come along. In the beginning it was more like fun, but then I became serious that I would make her come to End point with me. You know how stubborn I am."

"Yup I know that very well. Who doesn't know about your nature?" Kislay was smiling and I was again confused, whether it was a compliment or criticism. "Then what?" Kislay was more interested in my story than in my nature.

"You know she is very stubborn and she was adamant that she would not come. We kept on quarrelling till 9 pm, almost three hours. I was very much irritated by then. So I just said, "Ok you don't want to come, then it's fine. But remember, now I will have food only after having snacks with you at Shack Point."

"Oh my God, don't tell me you were serious. You were just trying EB on her. Isn't it?" EB means emotional blackmail or if I go by popular choice of Hindi speaking guys, EB means Emotional *Balatkar*. It's a short form we usually use in our college life.

"To be very frank Kislay, even I don't know why I said those words at that moment. I myself was not sure."

"Then when did you realize that you were serious and were actually not going to eat anything?" Kislay was becoming more and more inquisitive.

"Actually it didn't take much time for me to decide that I am going to keep my words. While I was returning to my hostel after that meeting, it was then that I decided I would really not eat until and unless Neelu comes to Shack Point with me."

"Oh, didn't she tell anything when you told her about your condition?"

"She said something like, don't be childish, grow up, why do you behave like an immature idiot sometimes, what point do you want to prove by taking me out to End Point?" Actually, I clearly remembered each and every word she said, but I did not want to reveal all those to Kislay. I remember every single line we spoke for those three hours. I have this problem. I can't forget things easily.

"Oh but how did all this end? Was she aware that you were actually not eating anything? Were you two in talking terms?" Kislay was full of questions. I never knew that he would be so much interested in my love life.

"Yes, we were talking to each other over the phone as we usually did at 10.30 pm but she was not aware of my fasting. She never asked me about that and I never told.

But Vicky and Shelly were suspicious that I was not eating food."

"That's what I was thinking. If you are not eating in mess, Vicky and Shelly will surely come to know as you three guys always used to hang out together." Kislay knew very well that Vicky was my roommate and we along with Shelly were closest of close friends. Almost all the times we used to be together. It was impossible to hide anything from those two.

"Whenever they asked me to come for food, I always said I would come later. They found it unusual, but on the first day they did not bothered much. It was on the second day that they smelled something fishy and compelled me to come to the mess. I had to tell them by force that I was not going to come and I did not want to discuss this matter."

"So they agreed?"

"Initially they did not, but they saw that I was too much disturbed. So they decided not to force me and make the matter worse."

"But then how did Neelu come to know about this? Did Vicky or Shelly tell Neelu?" My ciggie had finished. I lit a new one.

"Two days had passed. It was the third day, afternoon. I was feeling weak. We had our chemistry practical. I was in no mood to go but it was synthesis of Acetanilide."

"That's the most commonly asked one in the exams," Kislay told.

"I know. That's why I decided to go for practical. I wish I would have not gone. Hereafter the story becomes too embarrassing," I said with a laugh.

"Hey I know what happened next," Kislay was almost shouting. His voice echoed in the silence of End Point.

"You know?" Now it was my turn to be surprised.

"Yes I remember very well." Kislay was sounding confident.

"What do you remember?" Now it was my turn to be inquisitive.

"You fainted that day in the lab and were taken directly to KMC Hospital in Prof Mallikarjun's car. Vicky also accompanied you." Must say even Kislay doesn't forget things easily.

"Yes dear. The whole episode was too embarrassing." I fainting in the lab, all professors coming around me. Four of my batchmates taking me downstairs on a chair, Prof. Mallikarjun drove me to hospital. Everyone had a word or two to say.

"So now I know the reason why you fainted that day. I was watching that whole scene from the Pharmaceutics lab. We all were wondering how you fainted and that too in such a manner that you could not regain your senses and you had to be taken to the hospital. Now I understand it was because of that ailment which is defined as love and whose symptoms are sleepless nights and hunger strikes." Kislay was laughing madly. I also joined him. Yes, now I do laugh on these incidences. When Kislay's laugh meter came down he asked, "So Neelu must have rushed to the hospital on hearing this?"

"Hmmm no. When I was taken to the hospital, doctor found my stomach empty, blood pressure low, heart beat slow, even my haemoglobin was low". Doctor immediately told Vicky to give me some juice so that he could start the medications. So Vicky got some orange juice. But when he tried to feed me, I denied.

Kislay jumped from his seat, "Don't tell me. You were bed ridden in the hospital and still you denied eating and drinking. Were you mad?"

I was smiling, "Yes I was mad. You still don't know how much stubborn I am. Anyhow, Vicky was in total dilemma. He could not understand what to do. He told the doctor frankly that the patient was not willing to take food due to some personal problems. Doctor told that in that case he may have to start Glucose IV." Kislay looked really surprised, "So many things happened. We didn't have any clue."

"It was enough for Vicky. He called Neelu and asked whether I had any fight or argument with her. She simply denied. But asked, why Vicky is asking that. Vicky told her the whole story. He also said that I was not eating for past two or three days and even now when in hospital, I simply denied eating."

"That must have been enough for her. She must have come running to hospital," Kislay jumped to conclusion which was correct.

"Yup, she came to the hospital and we went directly to Shack Point from hospital."

"Wow so that was the story behind your first date with Neelu." Kislay was so happy, it seemed as he himself had dated Neelu. I saw the watch. It was almost 11 pm. "Kislay lets go *yar*. We will have something to eat at Parantha Point before going to hostel. I don't want to fast tonight." We both burst into laughter. On our way back, we were silent. I guess Kislay was busy analysing my foolishness and I was reliving those moments.

I could never forget that look of Neelu's face when she came to the hospital. She did not say even a single word, but that look revealed a lot. She was staring at me for about two minutes. In those two minutes I saw emotions of a lifetime. I saw guilt, I saw anger, I saw plea, I saw pain, I saw care and yes, I did saw love. Those two minutes are the moments that I can never forget in my life. The dinner was also memorable. The way she held my hands, the way she ordered for me, the way she served me and the way she fed me with her own hands are unforgettable. The taste of that dinner is still fresh in my memories and will always be. When you think of love, care and affection which Neelu showed, fast of three days seem to be nothing. But most memorable was our way back to hostel from Shack Point. We were walking closely. Cool breeze was blowing. Stars were smiling above. I could smell her aroma. Some of her hairs were kissing my cheek and sometimes my lips. We hadn't spoken a single word on our way back. When Neelu was entering inside LH she said, "You donkey! You are very precious and next time you try doing these types of stunts just think of your mom once."

"Akash are you still lost? Order something. We are getting late." Kislay dragged me back to the real world from the magic of my dream world. We ordered food and finished quick with normal conversations. We were inside the hostel before midnight. I was not too much worried about these timings. I had come late almost four days a week in B. Pharm and I knew how to manage the security personnel. But I had decided not to repeat those things in M.Pharm, at least I would try.

"Ok Akash, see you tomorrow in the college. Be on time and *yar* please keep guiding me about that new girl Simran." Kislay waved me to say good bye.

"Good night Kislay."

So, the name of that girl was Simran. I went to my room and opened my diary. I can't sleep before two. That's my problem. I can't sleep early and can't get up early as well. One of the major reasons of my shortage of attendance.

Introduction with Simran

* * *

Kukroo-Ko Kukroo-ko was the repeated cry of alarm set in my mobile. Alarm was set on repeat mode and I think it was repeating itself for the sixth or seventh time. "*Thak Thak*", I heard a bang on the door. I wondered who bothered to come so early in the morning. When I opened the door, I saw the guy who lives in the adjoining room. He was two years junior to me in some other course.

"Sir, can you please switch off your alarm. It's ringing for last half an hour and I am not able to concentrate on my studies. I have my papers," he said with a genuine request in his voice.

"Ya ya sure." I was a bit ashamed, but could not help it. I wonder what's the use of these alarms. It has never woke me up. Only time, I remember getting up by an alarm was when Vicky almost banged the alarm clock on my head. He would get irritated by waking up by the sound of my alarm and then make me get up. He threw the alarm clock on my bed one such day.

I did my daily chores like brushing, going to the

toilet, shaving as fast as possible and then rushed to college. As usual there was no time for breakfast. When I reached college, first lecture was almost over. I decided not to stand near my classroom. I didn't want to hear that dialogue again from the professor which I had been hearing for last four years, "Akash you are too early for the next lecture. Please come after ten minutes." I went to the canteen to have some tea and *upma*.

I did attend the lectures till afternoon. My new batchmates were maintaining distance from me. It was obvious that no one wanted to mingle with a guy who was praised so much by the Princi on the very first day. It did not bother me much though. In fact I was happy. I reckoned, it was a blessing in disguise. No extra burden of relationships for me, I thought. No interaction with anyone meant no intimacy and hence no friendship. I had learnt that relationships give nothing but pain, especially if it involves girls.

When I was coming out of the classroom, I saw Kislay, "Hey Kislay, coming to mess for lunch?" I was going to mess and thought I would get company during lunch. It's always good to have someone to talk to while eating in the mess. It is almost impossible to engulf the food of boy's mess without distracting yourself from the food.

Talking is the best way of distraction.

"You go ahead. I have to go to the market." Kislay said.

"Market? At this time? Anything urgent?" June is the hottest month of Manipal.Humidity is also high. A five minute walk is enough to get drenched in sweat. Students prefer to sit in the cosy air conditioned class rooms rather than roaming around and students like me prefer to doze off on the bed and sometimes even in the class room. No one likes to go out in the afternoons unless it's really important. Therefore, it was indeed surprising to see him skipping lunch and going to the market instead. As far as I knew, he was also quite lazy, may be not as much as me.

"Ya Akash, Simran has to do some shopping. So I have to accompany her." Kislay pointed to a girl standing beside him. That was the first time I noticed her. She was neither very modern nor very *Behanji* type. She was dressed in an orange coloured *salwar* suit with matching *duppata*. She had medium length hair which was coming till her shoulders. I noticed a small earring too. She wore a black watch and some kind of a band on her hand. The sandals were also matching with the *salwar*. Her face was small, round with a shade of cuteness. She had applied *kajal* on her eyes, which was actually looking quite cool on her because of her fair complexion.

"Actually she doesn't know anything about Manipal and it's the duty of old students like us to not let these new ones feel lost." Kislay continued. I guess Kislay had taken his lessons from our previous discussion and was right on button.

"Ya very true. You carry on…" I was interrupted.

"Hi. I am Simran. We are not officially introduced yet," Simran said with a smile and we shook hands. She had very tiny palms. I felt like I was shaking hands with an eleven year old girl.

"Akash here." I kept it as short as possible.

"I know you. Everyone here knows you." Simran still had that smile. I was trying to figure out the sarcasm behind that line and smile. I was expecting again to hear about my bunking capabilities, my carelessness, and my attitude. I was getting used to listening about these from my new batchmates. Everyone had done the same since orientation. But surprisingly Simran said nothing after that line. It was Kislay who said, "Shall we move?"

On our way out of college we talked about Manipal, its infrastructure, facilities, hostels, libraries etc. I let Kislay do most of the talking. When we were out of college, I said goodbye to both of them.

It is always difficult to attend the afternoon lectures after lunch. Stomach full means brain gets less supply of blood, which means brain becomes less active, which ultimately makes you feel sleepy, which means you can't attend lectures, which can even mean that you are sleeping on your bed.

"*Thak-thak thak-thak.*" Someone was knocking at the door. I looked at my mobile. It was 5 pm. There were three missed calls. All from Kislay.

"*Thak-thak*" my door was banged again. When I opened the door, it was he, who was smiling at me. I could clearly see the bubbles of happiness blooming in his eyes.

"Still sleeping?"Kislay asked.

"Still roaming?" Instead of replying I shot a question.

"Ya. We bunked afternoon classes for shopping.

We had a lot of fun." There was a continuous smile on Kislay's face.

"That's evident on your face. Let's go to the canteen. We will talk there." It was time for my tea and ciggie.

We started talking and Kislay couldn't be stopped.

"She was so flattered when I said it's my duty to take care of her. She said she was not expecting to find someone so caring, so far away from home. She is glad to have me as her friend. I think it's going to work. I will be dating her soon." Kislay was on cloud nine. I was amazed how he had come to that conclusion that early. I just said, "Good."

"It's all because of you. We bought so many things today. Right from a sim card to bed sheet, bucket to table cloth, notebooks to wafers. You name it, we bought it." Kislay was behaving as if he has found some hidden treasure.

I was kind of surprised. I had always visualized Kislay as a sensible guy. He might not have been very smart but he was not stupid either. But the way he was talking, I was compelled to think that he was a complete fool. I mean, how could a grown-up and a sensible guy be so happy on being a volunteer in shopping. There is something in these girls which makes guys lose their common sense.

"Akash please tell me what should be my next step?" Step, my foot! I had a strong urge to tell him, no matter what he did, he could never get any girl on earth to date. But why to shatter his bonhomie!

"Just spend as much time as possible with her. Make her feel that you are her only true friend in this place." Somehow, these words instantly came out of me.

Just then his mobile rang, "Hi Simran..."

I knew it's going to be a long conversation with Kislay trying to prove that he was her only true friend. So I decided to walk alone to the End Point.

First week was finished. As it was just the beginning of the session, there was not much pressure of classes and studies. We had a few theory lectures in the morning, but afternoons were generally free. I utilized that time in sleeping, playing carom and watching TV. Occasionally I visited CL (Central Library) mostly to surf net and sometimes to study. That is not to say out loud that I got interested in studies all of a sudden. I studied the things I loved studying, unfortunately not included in the course material. CL has a collection of more than ten thousand books and many international journals are available. It is a five storey building. I used to sit in some untraceable corner of the library and read few journals like HBR, Pub Med, Nature, Market Research, Market Analyst etc. I love business, advertising and marketing. These are the things that really fascinate me. I feel it's never easy to convince a person for any damn thing and when it comes to convincing someone to spend their hard earned money to purchase your product, the job is even more difficult. I always dreamt of taking that challenge. I always wanted to explore the psychological angle behind that "convincing process". Great idea to work upon. That's the reason I chose Pharmaceutical Marketing as my specialization in PG.

Almost all of my batchmates can be seen in CL. They are here in Manipal to study and that's what they are doing. Saikat with his typical studious look was expected to be here. But other guys like Bhusan, Fenil, Khan, Prateesh and Darshan were not lagging behind. Even someone like Bhagwan Din Pandey who could not even speak proper English and his I.Q, I can bet it is no more than that of a primary school student's, were also seen with thick foreign writer books all the time. Girls are always more sincere and the girls of my batch, were no exception. All the girls, be it Nishtha, Shefali or Shweta were in CL from day one. They would come here just after the college hours and stayed until midnight – because the library had to be closed at midnight. I sometimes wondered that at this rate they would finish the whole syllabus in just three months.

During my B.Pharm days I was a regular visitor to CL. But it had nothing to do with studies. It was more like a meeting place for chatting and bird watching. Who would not like to sit in an air conditioned lobby, sip coffee and have fun with friends and if I ever got bored sitting in a closed environment, I would simply go out and have a stroll beside the garden. A garden embellished with fountain and lights. If you were hungry and felt heavy in the pocket or had the privilege of NRI friends, you could have snacks in

CCD which is in the CL campus itself. In short, CL to me had always been a place to enjoy and unwind, rather than a place for serious study. Who would want to dip into boring books, when you have wonderful girls roaming around! You could see girls from almost every part of the world, from Blonde babes to Nigerian beauties, to north-eastern women and Malaysians to Burka clad Arabs. It's a sin if you ignore such beauties and immerse yourself in some nonsense book. In a nutshell, I was a frequent visitor to CL, but hardly ever bothered myself with the study section. I was wondering if I could find any guy with same mentality in M.Pharm batch at least. Seemed to be quite unlikely. Kislay could join me occasionally but I knew he couldn't be a regular lobby sitter.

I was sipping coffee sitting on the stairs of CL, when I heard a voice from behind.

"Hi Akash." It was Simran along with Kislay. He would hang out with Simran for as much time as he possibly could. In the last few days, he had really tried his level best to become a good friend of her.

"Hi Simran. So you liked this place Manipal?"

"Yes very much. It's a very nice, happening and interesting place. Much better than my previous college." The answer didn't surprise me. Whoever comes to Manipal falls in love with the beauty of it.

"I wish I had done my B.Pharm over here." Simran's voice was full of enthusiasm. Now that last statement was a bit too much for me. I know Manipal is lovely, awesome and people do get *senti* about this place. But in just a week, her likeness for Manipal had grown immensely.

"Come Akash let's go inside." Kislay was in no mood of standing there due to some obvious reason.

"No *yar*. You go. I am okay here. You know I hardly go beyond the lobby." I said and started laughing.

Kislay also laughed and said, "Ok we are going inside." That 'we' was interesting. It was an indication that Kislay had started taking decisions on Simran's behalf too. Of course I was fine with it. Besides I did not want to talk to Simran much. Did not want to create any wrong impression that I am eyeing his girl.

"I can't understand. You don't go beyond lobby, means you don't go to the study area. Then why do you come to the library." Simran was a bit confused.

"I come to the CL for fun. To meet and chat with friends, to have some relaxing moments in the garden, to sip coffee of CCD. I can't study those boring books all the time. I prefer to enjoy outside."I finished my coffee.

"Even I can't study much. Today I am coming to CL for the first time and that too because Kislay forced me."

Simran was sounding enthusiastic again. I don't know if that's her normal way of talking.

"I study only during exams. There are many things to do on this earth other than studying and we have only one life. Why to waste it in just mugging and studying. I don't mind losing out on a few extra percentages, but I want to enjoy life to its fullest." I could not believe what she said. Those were my feelings paraphrased by her. I was not expecting such a statement from a girl. Girls are always studious, career oriented and focused. But here was Simran, not giving a damn about studies. I don't know whether she was telling the truth or just trying to sound like me. If she really has this kind of carefree attitude then how did she crack the entrance of Manipal? She was either lying or was excessively intelligent. "Enjoyment is okay, but one should never neglect studies." Kislay spoke like a real well wisher of her.

"Yes Simran, Kislay is correct. You should not neglect your studies. You guys go inside. I will join you soon." I had to support Kislay.

"I never said that I neglected studies. I just said that I have my life outside this world, outside college, lab and library and I don't neglect them either. I know how to maintain a balance. I can't be talking and thinking of studies 24x7. But at the same time it doesn't mean that I would be bunking classes for no reason, like you do. I do know my priorities very well." Simran made her point very clear.

"So may I know what's on the top of your priority list right now?" I asked with sarcasm.

"There is nothing much to study as of now as regular classes have not started yet. And I don't believe in imbibing everything in one day. So I guess my priority would be to sit here and chat," Simran said with a giggle.

"That reminded me of the modified version of Newton's first law which we developed in second year of our B.Pharm. We often said that every book remains in state of rest or covered by dust unless and until an external force of exam acts upon it."

"Wow! What a thought! You seem to be a scientist. Just that direction of science is different." Simran started giggling again.

"We have to finish the assignment. Do you remember, Manthan sir gave it day before yesterday," Kislay interrupted.

I was not at all aware about any such assignment.
Obviously, it was given in the afternoon while
I must be busy sleeping.

"Oh yes. I had completely forgotten. I came here just to finish that assignment." Simran giggled again. This girl has a kid like innocence when she laughed. She is cute, really cute.

"Akash come, we will finish the assignment." Simran once again urged me to come inside.

"No *yar,* I was absent when this task was given.

So I need not do it." I am somewhat lazy when it comes to study.

"Leave him *yar*. He will not come. I have known him for last four years. He is not serious about studies. He can waste his time sipping coffee and watch birds going back to their nest. He can waste time accompanying juniors to Udupi, the nearby town. He can even waste time playing carom but he will never study." Kislay made his point very clear, so that at least now Simran would go in and finish the assignment.

Whatever Kislay said was correct, but it hurt me. Sometimes the way of speaking is more important than what you are actually speaking. I don't know whether he said it intentionally or not, but I was hurt. I was about to reply that, "Yes, I am waste of a person, who loves wasting his time." But in spite of me being so wasteful, I got 70% marks in B.Pharm, much more than what he could ever manage. Even in Manipal entrance exam, my rank was much higher than his. But I ignored. As I said before, I had learnt to ignore in B.Pharm.

I just said with a smile, "Ya dear you are right.

It's very difficult for me to study. You guys don't waste your time, otherwise you won't be able to finish the assignment."

Simran said, "Ok bye Akash. See you in college tomorrow. I hope you are coming. We will be having our first GD tomorrow." I had always loved discussions, but discussing something formally will be quite interesting, I thought.

"If I wake up on time, I will surely come," I said thinking about the torture of getting up early.

"Bye Akash," Kislay said to finish the conversation. While they were moving ahead, I heard Kislay saying,

"There are three varied types of students in Pharmacy. Some students make wonders happen. Some students see wonders happening around them and some students just wonder what's happening around them! I need not tell you who is in which category."

Kislay and Simran left, but grey matters of my brain were active and I was not thinking about Kislay's statement. I was very much accustomed to all these things. In fact, it was me along with Shelly and Vicky who had made this categorization after one of our booze sessions. I was just thinking about Simran who seemed to be so different. Yes it's too early to decide, but I can judge people very easily or at least I think that I can judge. She spoke directly from her heart. Whatever is inside her came directly out without any adulteration. It is one of the rare characteristics of girls. Usually girls never let you know that what's going on inside them. They have many faces or rather many masks over their face. They very well know which mask should be worn in front of people. Even the closest person never gets the opportunity to see the real face. Yes, sometimes you may feel that you have seen the real face of a girl. But that's the mask which you have seen and get confused with the real face. But Simran didn't appear to be wearing any mask or at least that's what I thought. My chain of thoughts was interrupted by a voice.

"Hi Akash. Sitting outside, all alone?" It was Khan, along with Nishtha. Those two were also always seen together. They had graduated from same B.Pharm College. No wonder they share a special bonding! Khan told that they were good friends in their undergraduate days. Nishtha being their batch topper has helped Khan a lot with his studies.

"Hi Khan! Hi Nishtha!" I greeted both of them.

"I was sitting here just to..." Nishtha interrupted

me.

"Don't be shy Akash. Just tell the truth that you have started bunking CL also, just like your classes. Now that you are in PG, there should be some progress. Enough of bunking college, now it's time to bunk CL!" Nishtha said and started laughing as if she had cracked a joke, which sounded funny only to her. Surprisingly Khan also joined in like the judge of any laughter show, where it's customary to laugh if your fellow judge is laughing, even if the joke is dead like a dodo. I thought probably Khan was trying to return some of Nishtha's favour pertaining to his studies. I have never seen him disagreeing with Nishtha on any matter. Either he is a very loyal friend or he is not a man enough. There is something in these girls that makes guys lose their common sense.

"Yes Nishtha you are correct. At least there should be something new. So I developed this new concept of bunking CL." I kept reminding myself, 'ignore Akash ignore'.

"Hey have you finished the assignment? We finished just now." Apparently Khan was trying to change the topic.

"No *yar*, I was absent when this assignment was given to us."

"So, what? During my B.Pharm I had never missed even a single assignment in four years," Nishtha said with a lot of self-pride.

"And all her assignments used to be the best in the class. I believe even here she will prepare the best one." Khan said it like one true loyal friend. It seemed like he was deeply indebted to Nishtha and didn't want to lose even a single opportunity to return the favour. "Why not! Once a topper, always a topper," I said with a spoof, which Nishtha noticed and said, “Let’s go Khan. It’s already 11.45 pm and I need to revise my assignment once before sleeping.”

“Good night Akash.” Khan said.

“Good night.” Nishtha said.

“Good night.” It was time to return to hostel after the sign off wishes for the day.

The Group Discussion (GD)

* * *

Next morning it was usual routine. That is,I got up late, skipped breakfast, reached college, only to find that I had already missed two lectures. It was break time of fifteen minutes before the start of the next lecture. When I reached the canteen, my batchmates were already there. After the customary greetings, I sat with them. They were all discussing assignments. It being their first assignment in Manipal, they were visibly – and understandably – excited.

Darshan was saying, "*Yar* I have never felt so insulted. You saw how sir threw the assignment on my face. I had worked for two days on that and he said it's all rubbish."

"Don't worry *yar*. We all are sailing in the same boat. I got E grade," Bhusan said in his typical Marathi accent.

"But worst comment was for *Bhagwan Din*." Fenil could not stop laughing. "Sir said that even his school going kid could prepare better assignment than this." We all burst into laughter.

"Not all got bad comments. Saikat was appreciated

quite a lot. He got an A grade." It was Prateesh this time.

"Yes but no one could match Nishtha." Spoke the greatest encomiast of all time. "I told she will prepare the best assignment and she has got an A plus." Everyone fell silent for a while. It was only Nishtha who was grinning and Khan smiling. "Come *yar*, let's move to classroom. It's almost time." Kislay reminded all of us about the forthcoming lecture.

On our way to the classroom I asked Kislay, "How much have you got?"

"I managed a B," Kislay said, sounding tad sad. He added, "But Simran got A." Kislay said with such pride as if he himself got an A. Perhaps, he has already started thinking of her as his girlfriend. But I was surprised that no one discussed Simran's grade.

The next two lectures were finished and we were walking back. Kislay and Simran were walking together. I deliberately maintained a distance of few steps from them. Just then, Simran looked back and saw me standing. She stopped and automatically Kislay stopped too.

"Hi Akash. Again bunked the morning lectures?" Simran said with a smile, rather laughing.

"Yes, same problem. I can't get up early,"I too replied with a smile.

"Early? Could you please tell me what your definition of early is?" Kislay did not seem to be in a good mood. May be he did not like Simran stopping to chat with me.

"Hmmm. That's a good question. Anything before 11 am is early for me." I gave the genuine answer. "Well Akash, don't bunk today's afternoon class.

We will have GD. Sir is already pissed off with you." Simran informed anxiously.

"Pissed off with me? Why? What have I done now?"I have not given him any reason to be upset with me.

"Yes you have not done anything and that's why he is pissed. Neither did you come on the day when he gave the assignment nor were you present on the day of submission," Kislay said as if he was pissed off more than the professor was.

"I see." I could not say anything more.

"LH has come". Simran said bye to both of us and we headed towards the mess. I was wondering whether my full stomach would allow me to go to college in the afternoon.

Life has become too monotonous in the past few days. Every afternoon this week, I have done the same thing, which is sleeping. Why not just change it today? I knew however, that if I went to my room I couldn't keep myself away from the bed. So after lunch, Kislay went to his room and I went to LP. LP is short form of Legal Point, which is the office of an advocate, close to police station. No I don't need any legal assistance. Actually, there is a small *dhaba* beside LP. As the *dhaba* doesn't have a name of its own, we call it LP. I decided to go there and have tea and ciggie to kill time.

I was on time for the afternoon classes. In fact I was early by fifteen minutes. I was told that afternoon lectures were held in a different classroom. Never in my B.Pharm days, had I ever entered that classroom as it was meant for PG students. When I opened the door I saw a totally different set up. It was quite different from our regular classroom. There was a podium and mike at one corner. One big table was placed at the centre and there were about twenty chairs around it. A few computers were kept at the back side. There was a big LCD screen and I could see it was wired with cable connection. Now that was too much for me! I have given few Power Point presentations on LCD, but I never knew my college had a cable connection as well. I was totally mesmerized by that ambience. For the first time in my life, I was eager for the class to start. I knew it was not going to be a regular lecture because chairs were arranged all around the table and not in a single line. It means no one can deliver lecture, because listening to lectures meant all the students had to look in one direction which was not possible sitting around a table. My batchmates came in one by one. We started chit chatting.

"Hey Akash,so good that you have come. I just met Manthan sir outside college. He was wondering that why you are not regular in class. Is there any problem?" Kislay informed me. Manthan sir is one of the youngest faculty members of our college, graduated from this college itself. It was on his suggestion that I opted for Pharmaceutical Management in PG.

Saikat was saying, "Sir has said that it was the easiest assignment that he could have given. Imagine what will happen when we will have to cope with tougher ones."

"Hey guys we have a guest appearance today. See who has come, Akash. We should all feel privileged to have him." Nishtha was best at humiliating.

"Ya ya, big people, big *fundas* of life, that's Akash." Khan had to add something.

The clock struck 2 pm and in came two of our faculty members, Mr. Manthan and Mr. Sridhar. It was for the first time I saw two people coming in to take a class.

After formalities of wishing each other, Manthan Sir asked us to sit.

He started, "It would be the first and last time when I will be speaking in this room. Henceforth, it will be you guys who have to do rest of the speaking. We will just listen to you all and at the end; we will share your marks and will also tell you about your flaws."

I was really happy. I love talking and discussing.

It's difficult for me to keep my mouth shut even for five minutes. I genuinely feel that the only gift God has given me is my way of speech. I guess it's only because of this power of words that girls get attracted towards me and I make so many friends easily. I am an expert when it comes to playing with words. I have been a fine orator since my school days. I won many prizes in debate, extempore and JAM in B.Pharm. May be that's why Manthan sir told me that I would be fit for Pharma Management.

For the next half an hour Manthan and Sridhar Sir explained us how to go about in the GD, as how to start it and continue , how to interrupt someone and how to disagree with someone. They also told us a few things about debate and extempore which would be held in the near future. Then they divided us in two groups of ten each. Both groups were given different topics and we were given ten minutes time to prepare. Marks were for individual performance and for the performance of the group as a whole.

The GD began. I don't know how I performed or how others performed. I was just too engrossed in the topic. All I knew is that I enjoyed those fifteen minutes. The topic was also one of my favourites-"Future of Animation in Pharma Industry". I had read a lot on that.

When both the groups finished, we were first told about our mistakes. They had noted down points of each student and were told individually about our deficiencies. Then they spoke about the shortcoming of the whole group. I found the whole session very productive and effective. For the first time, I felt that I have learnt something, not only from my teachers but from my batchmates also. Finally it was time to disclose individual marks. In the second group Nishtha, unsurprisingly, got the highest marks, whereas in my group I was adjudged the best. To say that, I was surprised would be an understatement. I never got maximum marks in my whole life, not even in kindergarten or even in any of the class tests or weekly exams. Marks never bothered me much, but for the first time I felt the pleasure of being at the top and it felt good. I had won many first prizes in co-curricular activities, but in studies,I never even dreamt of being remotely close to the top. It was a very different feeling and I was really amazed. I would never forget my first assignment and my first GD of PG – I bunked one and topped the other.

When the GD was finished and the professors left the classroom, Khan ran to Nishtha and congratulated with a smile that would have made him a perfect model for a Colgate toothpaste advertisement. "What a top class performance *yar*! You spellbound everyone. Your each and every point was so apt and logical. No one could defy you. You are simply the best." Khan was almost hugging Nishtha, as if she had won a gold medal in Olympics. I wondered whether Khan would now lift Nishtha up. Looking at his unrestrained excitement, it just seemed to be the next logical step. But I guess, in spite of all his excitement he was aware that it's difficult to lift an 80 plus package. So for now he was content to show his happiness by hugging and shouting. He couldn't risk his back after all.

"I have told you guys, she is the best in every field. If she can top in our B.Pharm college, she can top anywhere, in any field. No one can match her brilliance."Khan was still shouting. Actually Khan is not as stupid as he is behaving. He is quite good looking, smart and a sensible person. He is even good in studies and has pretty decent communication skills. He talks rationally, thinks rationally, and even behaves rationally only when it's something that does not involve Nishtha. His mind goes off track when there is anything related to Nishtha. May be I am wrong. May be he is well aware of what he is doing. May be that is the part of his plan. May be just like *Arjun* he is focusing on the eye of the bird. Or maybe just like every other guy, he also loses his common sense when there is a girl involved. Lots of 'May be's', who knows!

I also heard a few suppressed murmurs, "Sir is partial towards old Manipal students."

"Ya, I also think so."

"How can Akash top in GD?"

"If such non-serious guys can top, even my servant can top."

"Have you heard his accent, typical *Bihari.*"

I thought it's better to step away. I had enough of my batchmates rambling. I neither wanted to reply to them nor did I want to spoil my mood. I just ignored as always.

I was returning to my hostel. I was walking all alone as I was an out caste for my new batchmates. It didn't bother me much, as I myself was not interested in getting along much. Somehow I felt that my wavelength was not matching with them. It's better to be alone than to be in an uncomfortable company. Just then, I noticed Simran walking a few steps ahead of me. For a moment I was in a doubt whether to call her or not. Just now I was thinking that I need not mingle with anyone, then why the hell should I call her. Just a while ago I was thinking that my wavelength doesn't match with new batchmates, then why am I even bothered to call out to her. But I did call her, "Hey Simran, wait. I am coming."

She halted right there, with a smile on her face. Is she always smiling or her face is like that? I have always seen her smile, although I have not seen much of her.

"Hey! how come you are walking back alone? Where is Kislay?" That was the first thing I asked.

"He is in the college. He wanted to discuss with Sir about today's assignment and GD."

It means process of bottom licking and buttering has started. I know very well what we students try to do inside the cabin of our professors. Just try to score over fellow batchmates by hook or crook. It's all so disgusting, but it has become an integral part of our professional colleges.

"Why have you not accompanied Kislay? You could have learnt something." I spoke more out of sarcasm than anything else.

"No *yar*. It's just our first assignment and GD. We can learn and improve gradually. It's too early to discuss anything personally with Sir," Simran said very casually.

"And if I really have any problem, I can take tips from you. You seem to be good with GDs."She told with that same smile.

"I am not that good. It was just a fluke." I was not trying to be modest, I genuinely felt that.

"Even I am no genius to judge that but I saw you were so deeply involved, at least you were enjoying a lot."

"Ya, I do enjoy whenever I have to prove a thing or two. Moreover I like to prove others wrong. I love stating my point and holding tightly to it."

"I don't know whether it's a good quality or a bad one, but it shows that you have loads of confidence." Simran was unexpectedly talking serious stuff. As far as I know her, courtesy to Kislay, she is a very fun loving and bubbly kind of girl. I never expected her to talk anything remotely serious. At least that was the image portrayed by Kislay.

"Confidence is something that can take you places," she continued.

"Time to say bye *yar*. Your hostel has come," I said as we approached LH.

"Hey! Do you have any plans of going to the market?" Simran asked.

"No *yar*. I am going to the hostel. It's carom time for me. Bye."

I don't want to roam around shopping with her. Its absolute pain and only guys like Kislay could bear it. Also the information provided by Kislay has suggested that her shopping goes on for hours. It's a complete NO-NO for me. I can't waste my precious carom playing time for some nonsense shopping with a stupid girl. Hey hold on! Simran's shopping can be nonsense, but why am I calling her stupid? She has shown no sign of stupidity till now, at least not to me. Why am I categorizing her as stupid? Only because my batchmates say so? It has hardly been ten days, our batch has started, but almost everyone has been put under one bracket or the other. Saikat is categorized as studious scientist type of a guy who can only study and nothing else. Reason, I guess lies in his looks. He is bit bulky, wears specs, doesn't talk much, or even laugh much. He is somewhat self centred, a serious person. So he is categorized as studious, who is not good for anything except studies.

Darshan…categorized as comedian. Reason, he has a unique accent and whenever he speaks, it sounds funny. So, no matter how serious thoughts he puts forward, everybody just laughs and ignores him.

Bhusan is categorized as sex maniac. Reason, he asked someone whether there was any red light area over here. That question might be just out of curiosity, as he is from Pune which has a famous red light area called *Bhudwarpeth*. But he was looked upon as a sex starved creature and girls maintained a safe distance from him. Kislay was categorized as the most sober guy. Reason, no one has heard him speaking in a loud voice.

Simran was categorized as stupid or dumb. Reason, she talked very loudly, kept on laughing, never maintained a so called superiority which girls should have over boys. As far as I was concerned, I had already told that, I had been categorized as an outcaste. May be it was these categorizations which made me think that Simran was stupid. May be somewhere at the back of my mind I believed these categorizations were correct. It meant even I believe that I was an out caste for my batch.

Unforgettable Birthday

❄ ❄ ❄

First month was soon over. Nothing significant happened. I was back to my normal schedule of getting up late and bunking classes. I did participate in all GDs as they were in the afternoons and I could easily manage to attend college after getting up at 11 am. However, I could never repeat my performance of the first Group Discussion. One obvious reason for that was that mostly GDs were related to the topics discussed in class, which I never attended. Yes, I am good at playing with words, but one should have some knowledge of the topic and there need to be valid points to play around with. Most of the times, I lacked in-depth knowledge of the topic given to us. And yes, it was Nishtha who was the topper most of the times. Sometimes it was Saikat also.

It was evening, I was at the Legal Point, when Kislay joined me. I was surprised to see him. Mostly he is in the Central Library or with Simran during evenings. But of late, I have noticed that he is not spending that much time with Simran as he used to in the beginning. He has also stopped taking any kind of love tips from me.

"Hi Akash. When did you get up? I came to your room in the afternoon before going to college. You were fast asleep." Kislay sat down on the stool.

"Got up just now. I've just finished my tea and ciggie."I was wondering why Kislay came to my room, but I chose not ask anything.

"Akash, you should be serious about attendance. If you will have shortage again this time, be sure they will not allow you even for sessional." Kislay really seemed to be concerned. May be that's the reason he came to my room.

"I know *yar*. But I get really bored in those theory classes. GD and debates are ok, but listening to lectures for four hours is a big task for me."

"Just come for the sake of attendance. After all you need to write exams to get the degree. You can sleep even in classroom. I know you are an expert in that. You did that invariably during B.Pharm. I am still surprised how you slept without being noticed by the professors."

"That's my trade secret *yar*. I am not going to reveal that so easily. Anyway Kislay, I need to go now." I got up from my chair.

"Where are you going? May I come with you? I am getting bored."

"Bored? I can't believe! You have nice time pass these days." I started laughing.

"No Akash, really I am bored of her." I could not believe that Kislay got bored in just one month and that too without officially dating her even once. They were still following American system of payment. But I did not drag that topic much, as I did not want to create any misconception.

"I don't think you can accompany me to the place

where I am going now."

"Is there any such place in Manipal where I can't give you company?" Kislay asked surprisingly.

"I am going to score." I said it as calmly as I could have. Score is a kind of code word which we use to define the process of buying weed.

"Score? You still smoke grass?" Kislay was now more surprised. "I thought you don't smoke grass these days."

"Ya, I do occasionally. When *Bhole Shankar* wants to bless me, I have a round of *Ganja*. Today it will be first in PG." I laughed.

"There must be some special reason for this special feast?" Kislay was trying to digest the shock.

"Not really. Just like that."

"Hmmm. And who all are accompanying you? I am sure you will not smoke alone. You had a large gang in your B.Pharm days, especially in your final year."

"Gone are those days Kislay. There is no more gang. Yes, there are some juniors who smoke but I don't want to smoke with them."

"And may I know the reason behind that?"

"There are many but most importantly I don't want to be a regular smoker like them. If I smoke even once with them, they will pin me daily to have a drag. Then it might become difficult for me to resist."

"You don't want to smoke daily but you want to smoke just today? There must be some reason." Kislay, again to square one. But I just ignored his question. "I will go to End Point after scoring and smoke there all alone in peace."

"If you don't mind, may I intrude into your peace?"

"What? You also want to smoke?" I was obviously surprised. Kislay is a non-drinker and non-smoker. I can't even imagine him smoking ciggie, forget about grass.

"No *yar*. You know I never smoke or drink. I will just give you company."

"I don't need company. I am fine."

I thought Kislay was showing pity on me. If this guy doesn't smoke, what will he do sitting there with me!

"I know you are fine. I am coming with you as I have nothing else to do here and I am bored." Kislay insisted. It was the first time when I felt that Kislay was close to becoming a good friend.

"Okay then let's go. First we have to go to Lake View to score and then we will go to End Point." I paid the bill and we moved out.

It was twilight when we reached. It was pleasantly quiet, as most couples had already left. Cool breeze was blowing and sky was pretty clear with stars glaring at us. I always like to smoke in the open, in the arms of nature. I like to feel the vastness of the nature while smoking. We found a comfortable place and landed our butts. I bought two packets of chips and a bottle of coke, as one feels hungry after smoking and coke is required to wet the throat. You feel very thirsty and a peculiar type of irritation in the neck. Gulping any cold drink along with smoking helps to counteract that irritation. I took out Rizla paper and started rolling the joint. I rolled three joints at a time, as it's very painful to roll once you are already high. Kislay was sitting with quite a serious look. It was me who started the conversation, "Whenever you come here, you become very quiet. Why so?"

"Nothing like that *yar*. But I was just wondering that is it our curse or boon that we are here for two more years."

I guess Kislay's internal poet was surfacing out.

"All our friends have left this place. Some are busy

doing job, some are in other colleges. Why are we two left here? I miss those days so much." I had finished rolling and lighted my joint. After a few drags I started feeling light. Kislay was still continuing, "Why we human beings are so emotional? Why can't we think rationally? Why this mind can't accept simple fact that past can't be relived? Why the hell I am thinking so much?" Eventually Kislay stopped to sip coke. I was wondering whether Kislay was affected by passive smoking! There is no way that he will speak such stuff in normal frame of mind. I finished my first joint and lit the second one. I was smoking after a long gap and I was already feeling trippy. I looked up at the sky and the stars seem to be smiling at me and talking to each other. I could hear them whispering. I could not stare up for long. My head started spinning.

Kislay was talking non-stop. He was not at all bothered, whether I was listening or not, "You know these human relations are as intoxicating as your weed. First, you enjoy it, then it becomes your habit and in the end, it becomes a punishment. When you are high, there is no logic, no reasoning, and no fear. Similarly when you are at the peak of any relation there is no logic nor reasoning as well as and no fear of-course."I knew something has gone wrong with Kislay. But most amazingly for the first time I found Kislay talking some sense, although he was talking all nonsense. May be I lost my own reasoning power.

I was about to finish the second joint. I took a large puff and enjoyed watching the smoke coming out of my mouth and nose. My nearby vision was blurred by the cloud of smoke.

Behind that cloud, I could see some hazy obscure indistinctive images. Those images seem to be real, as if they all are standing in front of me. Slowly, the cloud of smoke faded and images became clear. They were all related to my B.Pharm. I could see Vicky riding on his bike. I was sitting on the pillion seat. We were driving real fast on Malpe beach.

I could see Dixa, my labmate of B.Pharm dissecting a frog.

"When will you learn to mount the heart? Who will do it in the exams for you?" I could see Amu running here and there with his nervous face holding notes in his hands and saying, "Hey bro, just two hours are left for University papers and I have revised just half the portion. I will flunk this time."

I could see Surya looking through his window at the Arabian Sea, pulling his hair slowly, as if trying to give them a spikes look.

I could see Anshuk applying Fair and Lovely cream on his face, expecting to get a milky white complexion in just fifteen days. Shelly was also sitting and asking, "Anshuk tell me, if we apply this cream on coal for fifteen continuous days, will the colour change to white?" Anshuk who was apparently pissed off replied, "This cream is meant for living creatures, not for non-living things. I believe that much science you must have studied."

Shelly was not short of words, he spoke up. "Ok you mean, if we apply this cream on black crow for fifteen days it will become fair like a Swan!"

I could see Aditya sitting in front of computer holding mouse in his hands but eyes closed. "Please wake up *yar*. We are almost done. Just two songs are left to record. We have to finish it tonight. Tomorrow is her birthday." I was excited.

Birthday Birthday Birthday, this word started echoing in my ears. All the images which were spinning around me,died out. I could just hear and feel only one thing, Birthday Birthday Birthday!

"You will light one more?" Kislay was saying something to me.

"What?" I was wondered where I was sitting. I was not even sure whether Kislay was an actual part of those images, which I was visualizing.

"You have already finished two joints. There is one more rolled up. So will you light that one also?" Kislay made his point clear. I was also clear that Kislay is really sitting with me and he is not part of those images. I sipped coke and started searching for matchstick. Kislay eventually found the matchstick and lit the last joint. As soon as silence made its presence, I started hearing Birthday Birthday Birthday.

I thought of talking something to distract myself. But my mind was empty. I could not think of any damn topic to discuss. That's what weed does. Just then, I remembered Kislay had come to my room in the afternoon. I got a topic, "Hey Kislay you didn't tell that why you came looking for me in the afternoon?"

"You want to know the real reason?" Kislay created unwanted suspense.

"Of course I want to know the real reason or else why would I ask?"

"I noticed that you were not in your usual self for last two days. You were…" I interrupted Kislay in between his expression of curiosity.

"What do you mean? I am perfectly ok. It's I who is smoking, but it's you who is losing sense. I am ok. I am ok." I kept murmuring. I knew I over reacted. Weed was showing its effect on me.

"I knew you would never accept that something is wrong with you. Actually I came to your room just to spend some time with you, so that you could feel good. I felt that you were lost in some other world for last two days. That's the reason I came here with you. I know you are missing your old B.Pharm friends. I know if one gets a company, he might feel good." I have never seen Kislay talking so intelligently before. May be weed is really showing its effect on me, otherwise how could I consider Kislay intelligent! Or may be passive smoking has made Kislay speak out his heart and definitely this guy is good at heart, for sure.

"Kislay, ups and downs are part and parcel of life. You can't be smiling all the time. You are correct. I am feeling a bit low for last two days." I mellowed down a bit. In fact Kislay's intelligent talk made me speak the truth.

"I am sure it's something to do with your past." Yet another intelligent remark by Kislay.

"You know a man is not killed by disease or illness. A man is killed by his memories, haunting memories to be specific." I took the last drag of my joint.

"I am sure that memory has something to do with Neelu." It was more of a question, than a statement by Kislay. I had to reply, "Yes, day before yesterday was her birthday."

"Then why are you sad? You should be happy for her, wherever she is now. Birthdays are the days of happiness and celebration, there is no scope for feeling sorrow or sorry on these days. In fact you should have celebrated her birthday."

Kislay said and started singing, "Happy birthday to you…"

I also joined in, "Happy birthday to you…" My mood totally changed. Few minutes ago I was sad, my heart full of pain and now I was smiling and singing. That's the effect of weed. Mood fluctuates too frequently. I felt so light that I started laughing like crazy, tossing my legs up and down. My laugh was echoing so violently in the peace at End Point that Kislay had to stop me, "Slow *yar* slow, otherwise security personnel might come." Kislay looked worried.

I eventually stopped laughing but still I was holding my stomach and was trying to catch my breath. Kislay too thought it was the weed's effect. "Are you okay Akash? What is so funny?"

"Actually there are two funny incidences related to Neelu's birthday. I just recalled those incidences and can't stop laughing. Sorry, if I scared you."

"It's ok, but you mind sharing those incidences?" Kislay obviously was interested to know about those incidences.

"First incidence happened when I was in first year and second, when I was in second year." I started peeping into my past.

"You mean those two incidences happened on two different birthdays?"

"Ya."

"Oh! Give me all the details." Kislay seems to be over exited and deeply interested.

"Wait *yar*. Let me roll last one. There is still some stuff left. I will smoke and tell you." I started rolling. It was difficult for me to see, the Rizla paper and stuff was falling out, rather than getting into the joint. I always hated rolling when I was high. Somehow I rolled the last joint. Kislay lit it without wasting any time. After two drags, I felt as if I had gone back to my first year, the evening before Neelu's birthday, "You know Kislay that time we were just friends. You may say good friends but not close friends. I was wondering what to gift her. I wanted my gift to be unique, memorable, and useful. Something, which can always remind her about me. I knew if I purchase something expensive she will never accept. So ornaments or watch was not an option. Teddy or soft toys are very common. Every second guy will gift that. Same is the case with chocolates and flowers. Yes, I can gift her a card with a poem written for her. No one else can give her that type of gift. It is not easy to write customized poems and by God's grace, I can write touchy poems. Therefore, I thought my best chance is to gift her card with a poem written by me for her. Then I thought we were just friends. Will it be correct to present her a poem now? Is this the correct time? Am I not going too fast? She may not like that idea at all, as it sounds too much personal. I finally dropped that idea. I was back to square one! It was already 8 pm and I was still in a soup." I stopped to sip coke as I felt my throat dry.

Kislay got the opportunity to speak, "How can a person think so much? I mean which normal person will spend hours thinking about just a gift. It's so unreal and if someone is putting so much of thoughts in each and every step of his Love saga, he deserves to be called a love *Guru*. Hats off to you, Love *Guru*!"

"It's not like that. We all think *yar*. I don't know why uselessly I have been given this tag of Love *Guru*." My irritation was obvious.

"I do nothing different from any other guy. Every guy tries to gift something unique to his girlfriend. If I was trying to do the same, what's the big deal?" I was loud and banged the coke bottle with a thud on the ground as I was pissed by hearing that word Love *Guru* once again. It was for sure effect of weed, which made me react so violently.

"Sorry *yar*, I never knew that you hate this tag. I thought you liked to be called as 'Love *Guru*'. I mean who will not! I would surely be on cloud nine if I manage to be even close to being called as Love *Guru*." Kislay tried to convince me that he did not mean to offend me by any means. "I am sorry *yar*, if you felt bad." His real concern was that with my spoiled mood I may not continue my story. But now I wanted to relive those moments. Even if Kislay would try to stop me, I would not. Weed has already taken me to my past life, most importantly,the sweet part of past. I took two more puffs and offered the packet of chips to Kislay. That gave Kislay an opportunity to speak, "But Akash,it's already eight, means all the shops were closed by that time. Although you had tomorrow's time in hand." "Same question Aditya also asked me." I rose from my world of trance.

"Aditya? Now, from where this Aditya came?" Kislay was unable to connect between Neelu's birthday and Aditya. Rather than answering his question I spoke whatever came to my mind. Weed had taken its toll and mind was not in my control any more. I just started speaking whatever thoughts lay inside me, "Yes, Aditya. You know he is the only person whom I have always considered more mature, sensible, more practical, and much more intelligent than me. Throughout my B.Pharm days, I had always listened to his suggestions and solutions. He was such a balanced guy, never saw him taking wrong decisions." I stopped for a puff and looked at Kislay. He plastered total confused look on his face. He asked rather hesitantly, "What's funny in this dude?

You told there was some funny incidence."

Now I recalled what I was speaking, "Ya ya. So you know it was almost 8 and I went to canteen, thinking that tea and ciggie might help to come to some decision." Kislay's face had an expression of 'thank God, he has come back to the point'. "In the canteen I met Aditya, who was swallowing his plain Maggi. Plain Maggi is nothing but Maggi boiled in water. I could never understand why anyone would like to have plain Maggi, when you can have vegetable Maggi with all kind of spices and onion at the same price. This guy's choice is so different." I was again losing my focus and speaking haphazardly. But Kislay was listening with a gentle smile. I could see canteen just in front of my eyes, courtesy effect of weed. Aditya and I were sitting in a corner.

Aditya asked me, "Where were you? Haven't seen you after college? You didn't even come to carom room?"

"I was in my room." I threw the gush of smoke out.

"Room? Entire evening in the room? What's the matter?" I told him all about my problem and the options I had thought of.

"You are correct. Poems are your USP. Don't show it so soon. But you need to be different. At the same time that gift should be in front of her eyes all the time."

"Ya I know- but my mind is jammed. I can't think of any such item. If I gift her teddy or any other soft toy it will always be in front of her eyes in her showcase. She likes soft toys a lot as all girls generally do."

"But that won't be unique," Aditya said promptly.

"I know. That's why I already dismissed that option."

"I think a gift should reflect that you know her very well. I mean something that can make her think that this guy knows the secrets of my heart, my likes, and dislikes." Aditya's mind was working fast.

"I know she loves chocolates a lot." I tried one option.

"That's not a secret. Every guy interested in her will know that." Aditya rejected that option too.

"What about a book? I know her favourite authors." I jumped with joy, as I was sure not many guys knew about her favourite writers.

"Book sounds too formal. Don't forget that you have to give a gift to a girl whom you want to date. There should be some essence of romance in that gift." Aditya rejected that option also.

"Oh Aditya, you are making me even more confused." I lighted another ciggie.

"Hey she is a nice singer. Right?" Aditya asked.

"Ya what's the big deal in that? Everyone in college knows that. She sung on cultural day. That's not a secret." I said with a dull voice.

"That's not a secret at all! What I want to say is that she must be interested in music and songs," Aditya said in a deep husky voice.

"Ya she is. So what, Aditya?" I still can't figure out, what was in his mind.

"Now tell me do you know some of her favourite songs?"Aditya asked.

"Ya I know quite a lot. She told many times during our conversation." I was still wondering what was in his mind.

"And think how many other guys know about her favourite songs? And even if they know, how many will remember them? I know about your memory. You can't forget things easily, especially if it is associated with Neelu." Aditya said with a wily smile.

"I am sure many guys are not aware of that. I guess Neelu doesn't discuss these things with many guys."

"Ya. That's it." Aditya banged his fist on the table. He continued, "I have an idea.

We will record one CD of all her favourite songs in it . It will be a nice gift."

"Wow! What an idea. It will not be expensive. It will be unique. It will be romantic with all those romantic songs she likes and most importantly, she will listen to it daily for sure. Who can resist a collection of their favourite songs?" I was almost shouting.

"Come, let's go. We have a lot of work to do. First of all we have to pen down all her favourite songs, then we have to decide the sequence of songs, then we have to download them from the internet and at the end we have to write the songs on the CD." Aditya sounded like a perfectionist with a beautifully crafted plan.

It was already ten. We went back to the hostel. Aditya had computer as well as internet connection. It took a lot of time to recall her favourite songs. At last we finished up with forty odd songs. Then we discussed thoroughly about the sequence. How first we have to set the mood, then we need to take her to dream world, then make her realize that I want to be a part of that world with her and at the end make her feel that I need her so very badly. We decided that this message has to be conveyed by means of sequence of her favourite songs, which means rejecting some of the pre-selected songs, thinking of another songs fulfilling that criteria and putting them in the right sequence. When we eventually finished short listing and sequencing the songs, it was already 2 am with two packets of Wills Navy Cut finished. I don't know who smoked more! But I do know that first song in that CD was 'Ek *din aap yun humko mil jaenge*' from the movie 'Yes Boss' and last song was '*Jab koi bat bigar jae*' from the movie '*Jurm*'.

"Akash I am real sleepy now. Can we please complete rest of the work tomorrow?"Aditya said with his bloody red eyes. I remained silent. Looking at Aditya's face I could not say anything.

"Tell me *yar*. Shall we do it tomorrow? I am sure you will not be meeting her before evening. We can bunk afternoon classes and finish rest of the work," Aditya said yawning badly.

"Actually I am meeting her in the afternoon between 1 pm to 2 pm during lunch time." "Are you crazy? You couldn't get any better odd time than this?" Aditya was losing his temper.

"I can't help it *yar*. In the evening, her South Indian friends from MIT are coming to visit her. At night she is going for dinner and cake cutting with her batchmates." I passed him the information.

"And of course she cannot invite you either with her MIT friends or her batchmates. You are class apart." I could sense the sarcasm in that last line, but I knew it was more out of frustration of losing on sleep than anything else was.

"You Know *yar*, I sleep early. I can't even keep my eyes open." Aditya said with a lot of pity. His eyes looked very small because of the burden of sleep. I could see water coming out of his eyes due to irritation. But even then I kept quiet. It was Aditya who spoke again, "Don't worry. We will finish it before afternoon. I will bunk morning classes and I don't think you have any problem in bunking."

"I think you are forgetting something. Tomorrow we have our practical viva and no way can we bunk college." I was rather hesitant, expecting a blast from Aditya.

"Oh viva! You know I have read that somewhere, 'Silence is the best answer for all questions' and 'Smiling is the best reaction in all situations' but unfortunately neither of them helps in viva." Aditya as always was about to start his lecture regarding viva and practicals. I was praying that his mind comes back to recording, rather than thinking about viva. I think God was somewhere close to me.

"Oh! It means we have to finish recording now only." Aditya did not even blast out. I guess he rejected to the adversary of the situation. "Ok let's get on with it." Aditya almost shouted the last line, as if trying to keep himself awake. I pity him but I was helpless. It was his idea and anyhow he has to do it now. He cannot leave me in between. After all it would be my first gift to Neelu. For a moment I thought that I would do rest of the work myself, but then my knowledge of computers is as good as Rabri Devi's knowledge of Indian economy. For me computers are like rocket science. I cannot even prepare a Power Point presentation, forget about CD writing.

"Pass me a ciggie dude," Aditya said while looking at the computer screen.

"It's all finished." I pointed at the empty boxes of Wills Navy Cut.

Aditya did not utter a single word, but gave me a look as if he would swallow me without delay. I just dug myself into a magazine. When I looked up I saw Aditya was looking at the computer screen. I was relieved that he is working. After some time I looked at him again. He was still looking at the computer screen and there was no change in his posture. I went closer to him. My God! He was holding the mouse in one hand, but his eyes were shut. He had dozed off. I stood there for about two minutes. There was no movement and no signs of Aditya getting up. I shook his shoulders. Aditya got up, "What's happening here? What are you doing here so late, at night?" Aditya seemed to have lost connection from this world as he was roaming in his dream world for past few minutes.

"Hey Adi, we are doing this CD thing to gift Neelu. Don't you remember?" I deliberately called him by his nickname just to show my closeness. That's the only way I could have justified my torture.

"Oh Ya. Ok let's get on with it." Aditya shouted

again. I doubted how much he can get on now. After about five minutes it was again the same scene. Aditya dozing off with mouse in his hand and his face towards the computer screen. I again woke him up. This process was repeated for about five to six times. Each time I woke Aditya up, he said the same line, "Ok let's get on with it."

Eventually at 4 am we were done. I was indebted to him for his help. I just said,

"Thanks *yar*. I will never forget your help..." I was interrupted in between by Aditya,"Hey come on. It was really my pleasure. After all I am Abdullah."

"Abdullah??? What do you mean *yar*?" I was very close friend of Aditya, but had never heard this one liner from him.

"You have not heard that famous song of Raj Kapoor from the movie '*Jis desh me ganga behti hai*'?" Aditya just gave half information.

"I have watched that movie long ago on Doordarshan, but which song are you talking about?"

"'*Begani shadi me Abdullah deewana*'. I am that Abdullah," Aditya said that and started laughing. I too joined him.

Kislay also started laughing who was deeply engrossed in my story. He said, "I can't believe Aditya called himself Abdullah and he slept on the computer, that too not once or twice but about six times. It's really funny Akash."

"I know *yar* its funny. But you know, I have made my friends suffer a lot." I got a little emotional. Weed always make me emotional.

"What about the second funny incident?" Kislay has not forgotten about that.

"Look at the time. We need to rush to the hostel now. Let it be for some other time."

"Some other time means tomorrow?" Kislay was

very enthusiastic to know.

"No *yar*, not tomorrow. May be when I am smoking grass again. Or may be… I am not sure *yar*." I rose to stand up. It was difficult to walk after so much of grass. Kislay did support me.

Tea with Simran

❄ ❄ ❄

It was impossible for me to get up in the morning after that heavy dose of weed. I got up at lunchtime, went to the mess, then to college. I saw Manthan Sir parking his car,

"Good Afternoon Sir!"

"Good Afternoon Akash. I wish you could wish me good morning someday." Sir said with a smile on his face, which is so typical of him. He is always like this, full of fun and wit, but when it comes to lectures, he is one of the best.

"I am trying my best sir."

"Akash, you really need to be serious. We have clear instructions from Principal that if there is attendance shortage students won't be allowed even for sessional exams. I don't know what's your problem? Why are you trying to screw your future?" I held my head down. I really didn't have any answer. I know that my logic of getting bored in theory classes is not a valid excuse.

"Still you have time Akash. You can make up for

your lost attendance, if you are regular henceforth.

You should respect the rules and regulations." Sir was sounding very firm. It means it's high time.

"Sir I will try, really."

"Ok Akash." Manthan sir went to his cabin.

I was standing, stranded thinking what would happen if I were not allowed to appear for exams. I was thinking whether I would ever overcome my laziness and make myself ready for mental torture in classrooms. In B.Pharm, it was for my friends, especially my roommate Vicky who used to force me to attend classes. It was a part of Vicky's rountine to wake me up, which included a lot of shouting and shaking. He even had to kick my ass to wake me up. But never left me sleeping. Then we used to rush to the college on his bike. I still wonder how he was never fed up with waking me up daily. But now Vicky is not here to kick my ass. I entered the classroom. I came to know that today a debate would be conducted, which was announced in the morning classes. My batchmates were enthusiastic yet again. They always show a lot of interest when something new happened, which was quite natural. I don't know why I never feel any enthusiasm for any damn thing.

"We will be paired together. One will be speaking for the motion and the other, against." Saikat was explaining to Darshan.

"Well the topic will be same for everyone?" Bhusan intervened.

"Yes topic will be same for every team and Sir has precisely told that there should not be any repetition of points. If we repeat the points, our marks will be deducted," Saikat said again.

"It means those who are speaking at the beginning will have an edge," Khan said. "Don't forget that those who are speaking in the beginning will have lesser time to prepare." Kislay kept his opinion.

"But how will the pairing be decided?" That was the first question I asked.

"That will be according to a lottery system. Sir will give a number to each one of us; whoever gets the same number will be paired,"

Saikat explained.

"Marks will be awarded to teams, not to individuals. Gods knows what will happen if I have to pair with Bhagwan Din Pandey!" Nishtha looked worried, as if she had to swallow a snake.

Just then,the bell rang and entered Manthan Sir and Sridhar Sir. Manthan Sir said, "Come here one by one and pick one chit. It has a number in it. Find your matching number and sit with your partner." We took the chits. Nishtha was paired with Khan. Saikat was with Kislay. Prateesh was with Darshan. I was paired with Simran. I did not bother to notice the other pairings.

Sridhar sir said, "Teams will come according to their numbers. Those who have got number one will come first, followed by second. You get fifteen minutes to prepare and then we will start the debate."

"Here is your topic," Manthan Sir said writing on the board.

Topic was "GATT will boast up Indian Pharma Industry". It has been a hot topic since quite some days. Everywhere from News channels to newspapers, there were discussions on GATT and its consequences. And most of us believed that it's not going to be too good for Indian Pharma Industry.

All of us sat with our respective pairs and started discussing the topic. I saw Nishtha sitting with Khan. She looked overjoyed, as if she had found some hidden treasure. Khan also looked very satisfied with his 80 kg baggage! "Hey Akash, you going to speak for the motion or against the motion?" Simran enquired.

"Whatever you say. I am comfortable with both." I was really not sure, whether I wanted to speak for or against.

"Listen *yar*. I don't have much idea about this topic. You have to tell the points, both for and against. So it really doesn't matter to me whether I am speaking for or against." Simran was having that kid like smile on her face. I was stranded for a few seconds. How bluntly she accepted the fact that she did not know much. There are very few people who have the guts to accept their weakness. Generally, we want to show ourselves much more intelligent than what we actually are, and here is a girl who has no inhibitions to accept the truth.

"What are you thinking? Tell me the points. We should pen it down." My thoughts were disrupted by Simran.

"Ya sure. Let's have at least ten solid points both for and against. Once we have the points ready, then we will decide that who will speak for and who will speak against."

"And remember that our number is fifth. So we may have to change some points, which will be covered by other teams. It's better to have fifteen points, rather than ten," Simran suggested.

"Okay. Let's first discuss the 'for' points." "Akash, I think first we should speak a little about the influence of GATT on international level and then we should put it in Indian context."

This girl had a thinking cap. "Sure Simran that will be good."

I wrote a few points. Just then Simran spoke again, "Will it be okay if we put a bit of history of GATT. If we mention the year of its formation and year of replacement, it may sound better. Figures always have a value addition."

"That will be fine, but I don't remember the exact dates."

"GATT was signed on 1st January 1948 by 23 countries," Simran told promptly. I could not stop myself, "Just now you said that you don't have any idea about this topic, but on the contrary you know a lot." "These all things are very common in newspapers and I do read it daily," she said with that same sizzling baby smile.

We prepared our debate in fifteen minutes. I must confess that Simran underestimated herself a lot. She was having a lot of knowledge about this topic. May be she was just trying to be modest. It was decided that I would speak for the motion and she speak against the motion.

One by one, we started speaking. Soon it was our turn. I spoke first for the motion. I have done this all through my B.Pharm. Speaking on stage is my hobby, my passion, my love. I am a completely changed person when I am on stage. I won so many prizes at many different levels that I really enjoy debating. It was due to these extra-curricular activities, that in spite of me being so irregular in lectures and practical, I was quite popular. Here it was a serious debate, but after all it was a debate. I spoke non-stop for five minutes and I knew that I spoke well. All my batchmates were surprised, except Kislay. Nishtha was shaking her head in disbelieve, which reconfirmed that I have spoken well. I looked at Simran who was sizzling with her smile. Now it was her turn to speak. She was not a very good orator, but she spoke well within her limits. She could not modulate her voice as I could, nor she could use her body language along with facial expressions, but she spoke in a balanced manner. Saikat also spoke well, but the problem was that his voice was not very clear and had that typical Bengali accent which made his English sound a bit funny. Nevertheless his points were very good and the way they came in a sequence was good too. Then came the pair, Nishtha and Khan. Deep inside my heart I was waiting to listen to her. I had heard so much about her in this past one month that I was curious. Although I have heard her in GDs, but taking part in a GD and speaking in a debate is totally different. She spoke in flawless English, perfect accent. Even her voice modulation, pause, aggression and dramatization were also good. No doubt she was the topper. Even Khan spoke well. Not as good as Nishtha, but he was better than the other batchmates. Eventually debate came to an end. As customary, Sir told us about our mistakes and discussed the points which we have missed. At the end, Sir told the marks of each team. Nishtha and Khan were on top, which was not a surprise at all. But the thing which was surprising is that team, Simran and Akash is just next to Nishtha and Khan. It was quite obvious that whole evening my batchmates in CL were busy discussing that how come a pair of an out caste guy and a stupid girl could be second topper! While my batchmates were losing their hunger thinking about us, we two were sipping coffee in Santhala. Santhala is a South Indian restaurant, which serves typical dishes like *Idli, Dosa, Uthaapa*, and *Vada* etc. We usually have tea or coffee there, as any other solid food is difficult to engulf. It so happened that after college all our batchmates dispersed without even bothering to say a formal bye. Even Kislay did not come up to Simran. Apparently he was also upset. Showing friendship or acting as a friend is totally different from being a true friend. He was also a bit shattered from the outcome of the debate. So, it was just two of us left alone. Actually we did not even notice that no one was talking to us. We were happy about the debate. Success in studies was a rare commodity for me and I was ecstatic. Simran was also very chirpy. As a matter of fact she is always chirpy. Just that, now she was even chirpier.

"Akash, that was some kind of oration. How come you are so expressive! You just nailed it *yar*." Simran was almost shouting on our way back from college.

"I have been participating in debates since my school days. I know a few tricks to impress the judges."

I began laughing.

"Now I know why Manthan Sir said that you are not justifying your potentials."

"When did Sir say this?" It was new information for me.

"Some days back, in a theory class he said during roll call."

"But why he said that?" I was still not able to figure out the reason of that statement.

"Actually Sir called out your roll number twice and someone answered-absent. Then Nishtha added 'as usual' to that. Everyone started laughing."

"Huh." I said as if I didn't care about their laughs.

"Then Sir said, you all should laugh. A guy who is not doing justice to his potentials should be a laughing stock. He deserves to be a laughing material." Simran stopped suddenly. She must have noticed the change on my face. I did not know how to react. Whatever Sir said was absolutely correct. If I am not serious about lectures, these types of comments will come and I should not feel bad. I have chosen this kind of college life and I cannot shed away from its consequences.

We reached LH. I was about to say bye, when Simran said, "Oh it's already 5.30. Debate took so long to finish. Now my mess is closed. No evening snacks for me and I am hungry like hell." Again that innocence emerged on her face. It's difficult to ignore that innocence.

"What is the closing time of your mess?" Simran enquired.

"Its 5...I guess or may be 5.30. Actually I don't go to mess in the evenings. I go to canteen."

"Will it be open now? I need to eat something."
"I think there is a canteen inside your hostel too." I knew there was a canteen inside LH.

"Yes, but it has only biscuits, ice cold samosas and machine tea. I don't drink machine tea."

"Well in that case we can go to Santhala. You can have nice tea there." The moment I said that, I regretted. It's been long I have been to Santhala with any girl and I really did not want to.

"Where is Santhala?" Simran asked. I was surprised. How come Kislay had not taken her to Santhala! May be he might have felt that Santhala is below his standard. Some guys think that expensive restaurants can impress girls.

"It's near TC." I said.

"TC means Tiger Circle. Right? It's just five minute distance from here!"

Simran also looked surprised. "Yes it's very near."

"Okay then let's go."

We ordered some *pakodas* to eat. After *pakodas* it was time for tea. I was a regular customer of Santhala. It was the regular chit chatting spot of ciggie and tea-loving guys like us in B.Pharm. The owner and all the waiters there knew me very well. It was customary that whenever our group sits there, we were served tea and Wills Navy Cut without even asking. But today, the waiter was in doubt whether to serve ciggie or not, as I was with a new person, that too a girl. Even I was in a doubt whether to smoke or not, although I had a strong urge to smoke.

It was like a routine for me to smoke ciggie and

drink tea in evening after college. I made up my mind. I will not pretend anything in front of this girl. And why should I! I don't give a damn about my reputation. I am not at all bothered if she becomes my friend or not. So why should I be thinking about her reaction about my smoking. If she wants to be my friend, I should be the way I am.

I said, "Simran, do you mind if I smoke a ciggie. Actually, I smoke and with tea I need it badly."

"It's ok." Simran kept it short and simple. I tried to read the expressions on her face, but then thought that why I am taking so much trouble. She has said ok, so just smoke *yar*. Forget about what's going on in her mind. That's none of your business. I just gestured the waiter that I needed a ciggie and he got it in a flash. Simran looked a bit surprised, that how without me saying anything;the waiter got me my brand of ciggie. With a few puffs in I started the conversation.

"Don't be so surprised. I have been here for four years and this was our *adda* in B. Pharm. Waiter knows me very well and my brand also."I pointed at my ciggie.

"So you are a chain smoker?" "No. I don't smoke that much."

"Kislay has told me many things about your B. Pharm batch. I know that you smoke."

It was not a surprise at all that Kislay had already praised my virtues.

"What else did he say?"

"Nothing much. But yes he has told that you were more regular in college during UG. In M.Pharm you have become more careless. Ideally it should have been reverse of it."

"Ideal things never happen." I don't know why I said that.

"Hey 'Ideal' reminds me of something, why didn't you come for the movie 'Ideal Partners' on Saturday? All our batchmates were there. You knew that we all were going for that movie. Right?"

"Yes, I knew and that's why I did not come. I don't know why but I just can't be comfortable with my new batchmates. I just don't like their company. They are not of my type. My old batchmates were too good and somehow my wavelength is not matching with my new batchmates." I stopped to take a puff of ciggie.

"You mean to say that your current batchmates are disgusting fools who are boring?" Simran seems to be annoyed by my comments. After all she is also my new batchmate and she might have taken my comments personally.

"No *yar*. They may be as intelligent as Albert Einstein and as happening as MJ or JL. But my thinking doesn't match with them. I don't feel like even talking to them. So why should I come for the movie?" My voice level had increased alarmingly. I took two puffs of ciggie at a time. Simran was looking at me with wide eyes. I thought for sure she was going to shout back, as without any reason I had shown my temper.

"Who are MJ and JL?" Simran asked with her childish innocence. That was total reverse from my expectation. I could not stop myself from smiling.

"MJ is Michael Jackson and JL is Jennifer Lopez." All my hot temper vanished just in a second.

"I see. You know, that day I asked Kislay why you hadn't come for movie. He said that you don't like to socialize. That time only I though, there was some problem."

"Simran you know I am a movie buff and I didn't want to spoil my movie experience with those guys. That's why I decided it's better to avoid and Kislay is correct I don't socialize where I am not at ease."

"Hey even I like movies too much. I seldom miss any movie." That was one common hobby of us, which made us good friend in the coming days.

"Yes but in Manipal there is no movie hall, forget about multiplexes. Here you will get only DVD theatres."

"DVD theatres? What's that?"

"It's the hall where movie is played on the DVD player and shown on LCD screen. If the movie is a new release, then mostly it's a pirated DVD."

"Oh, then the picture quality must be bad. It means last four years you have only seen pirated movies." Simran giggled with her same kid like innocence.

"Sometimes we go to a nearby town Udupi, if there is some real good movie. But problem is that they don't play Hindi movie very often. They are obsessed by their Kannada movies."

"Is that a multiplex?"

"It's not your Delhi. It's just a small town and it's a simple theatre."

"What you mean by my Delhi? I am not from Delhi. I am form Karnal, Haryana."

"Oh."I just exclaimed.

"And before you get it wrong again, let me tell you that I have done B.Pharm from Hindu College of Pharmacy."

"Ok."

"And mine was a small college. It's not as big and as happening as Manipal. Even the town is very small. That's why we used to fly away to Delhi on any excuse."

"Oh."

"My previous college was so dull. Only good thing was my friends Divya, Sapna, Meenakshi. It was so much fun with them. There was not even a single guy who we had not bullied. Once we even beat a guy."

I was taken aback by the information over load. Was she trying to scare me? But she was smiling as always. By her expressions it was obvious that she was in no mood of scaring me. She continued speaking. "You know, Divya and I were called *Aaj Tak* Channel."

"*Aaj Tak*! Why the hell you two got that name?" I was very surprised. "We had the news of all the happenings in our campus, whether it's a proposal by any guy, dumping of BF by any girl , internal fight within the hostels, scolding of lecturers, we were always aware of all."

"I see."

"You know we four were roommates. It was a four seater. We used to chat till late in the night, almost till 4 am. We used to laugh so much and so loud that our next door girls could not sleep. They used to come daily requesting us to be a little softer while talking and laughing. But we never listened to anyone. We did whatever we liked." Simran spoke everything in one go, as if there is no tomorrow. I was thinking even I was like that in B.Pharm. We also used to chat until late night and used to disturb the top floor by shouting and laughing. Even after many complaints from other students to hostel warden, there was no change in our nightlife.

Simran was still continuing, "Our group was like a threat for other girls, especially for juniors whom we ragged so much." This girl is a real chatter box. I have never really appreciated company of such girls who talk a lot, although I myself talk a lot. But I don't know why I was not irritated by Simran's constant chat. I could not make out any obvious reason for that. May be because I liked her innocence, may be because her constant smile made me happy, may be because she was a movie buff like me, may be because she also had a happening group like me in B.Pharm, or may be because she is the only person who has spent some time with me. Don't forget that if I don't want to mingle with my batchmates, even they treat me as an outcaste. So I may be enjoying my moment of attention. In the mean time, I had taken two more cups of tea and Wills. It was already 8 pm.

"Shall we make a move now? It's already dinner time *yar*." I paid the waiter.

"How much is the bill?" Simran asked. I knew it was coming. She will now insist on paying the half bill.

"Simran I know you want to split the bill. I don't mind that. You may pay the whole bill. But not this time *yar*. Next time around do whatever you want to do."

"Ok, not an issue. See you tomorrow morning. Are you coming for the lecture?"

That's the most dreaded question, simply because I don't have an answer, "I am not very sure." We got up and started to walk towards hostel.

"What's your problem Akash? Why can't you come?"

There were so many reasons, but I did not want to reveal all that. I simply said, "I can't get up."

"You don't have an alarm clock?"An obvious question.

"I can't get up by alarm clock." That may sound ridiculous, but that was true.

"So how you used to manage in your B.Pharm days?"

"My *roomy* Vicky used to wake me up. He is in NIPER now, doing his M.Pharm there."

"So who is your roommate now?" "I am staying in a single seater."

"Then you should have stayed in a double seater. Kislay could have been your roommate," Simran suggested.

I wanted to say that I could not even imagine anyone except Vicky as my *roomy*. We had such a bonding.

We compliment each other so well and our understanding level was so good that for all four years we were together in the same room. We never ever thought of changing the room. Even in final year when most of the guys were moving to single seater to concentrate on studies so that they can qualify GATE, we decided to be together. Now I don't want to spoil such nice memories by having some stupid guy as my roommate. Moreover I knew very well that it's not easy for any person to stay with me, bear me, and tolerate me. My mood fluctuations are very unpredictable and everyone can't be Vicky. So I deliberately decided to stay in a single seater. But it was too soon to share these things with Simran. I said, "I wanted to stay alone *yar*. Don't want anyone to disturb me, when I am sleeping."I laughed and so did Simran.

"How much time do you take to get ready?" Simran was ready with her next question. We had already reached the diversion from where we had to move in opposite directions. But Simran was talkative as ever.

"It depends. If I am getting late, ten minutes are enough. If I have time, then half an hour."

"I see."

"Simran lets move. It's almost nine. Our mess will close."

"The food is yuck."Simran said with an expression of throwing up.

"You are in South India. What do you expect? Typical Punjabi food?"

"My roommate told me that food of BQ mess is good."

"I too heard the same."

"What you mean by heard? You have never eaten there? I thought you have been to all the places in Manipal in last four years."

"No Simran, I have never eaten there, neither in BQ mess nor in BQ canteen."

"Ok Akash. It's getting late. Mess will close. See you tomorrow." Simran started to walk.

Just then I heard Simran calling me, "Akash wait a minute."

"What happened?"I asked.

"It's been a month here and I still don't have your mobile number."

"Even I don't have your number. Never got an opportunity to talk to you so much. My number is 9858682021. Give me a miss call so that I can also have your number."

"Ya ok and final good night."

On my way to boy's mess I was thinking about BQ. Actually there are three big messes in Manipal. One is the boy's mess which is inside boy's hostel, second one is lady's mess which is inside lady's hostel, third one is BQ mess which is inside BQ hostel. BQ mess is common for boys and girls. It's actually a mess for couples. All the couples join this mess, so that they can have food together. It sounds so romantic. It's not like, singles don't join this mess. But it's very rare. It feels so odd with couples sitting all around you, looking into each other's eyes, serving food for each other, laughing, smiling and getting lost in their own world. A person who is alone feels so out of place in such an atmosphere. I was kind of alone in my B.Pharm days in terms of having a genuine girlfriend. Neelu would obviously never come out to eat in this place with me. Taking her out for a single dinner made me fast for almost two days. Making her join BQ mess for a month meant that I would have to fast for one year. So I never had the guts to ask her. Neither had I any friend, obviously a girl who was so close with whom food can be taken daily without getting bored. So I never ate in BQ mess. Same was true for

BQ canteen. I reached my mess. There I met Kislay. "Hey Akash. Where have you been? You were not seen anywhere, neither in carom room, nor in canteen."

"I was with Simran in Santhala."I replied as if I had committed some crime. I knew Kislay would not appreciate me hanging out with Simran.

"Okay *yar*." Kislay was surprisingly cool. We finished our dinner. Kislay went to CL to have his dose of mugging and I went to carom room. I was done playing carom about 12 in the night. Then went to my room and started reading "Consumer Behavior", the book which I had issued from CL. I don't know when I slept.

AIDA Model

* * *

Duniya hasino ka mela, mele me ye dil akela...I heard the ring tone of my mobile. I was annoyed as my sleep was disturbed. I put the pillow over my ear and tried to sleep. I was sure whoever is calling will not call again. My mobile rang again...*Duniya hasino kamela, mele me ye dil akela*. I ignored again. But when my mobile rang for the fourth time I had to get up. I reached my mobile, thinking of all the curses for the caller. When I read the flashing name, I was astonished. It was Simran. I answered the call.

"What happened Simran? Calling so early? Must be something real urgent." I was yawning very badly.

"It's not early. It's already 8 am and now that you have got up, get ready and come to college. You have enough time. So you can take half an hour to get ready." Simran started giggling again.

"What the hell is this? You have called to wake me up?" Rather than being thankful, I was irritated. Actually I was not expecting this call and I did not know how to react.

"You only said that you can't get up on your own.

Now don't waste your time and mine too. Even I need to get ready. See you in college. Bye." I sat on my bed for few minutes without moving.

I had a strong urge to sleep again. My bed was too tempting, hard to leave. But somehow I resisted. If I have got up, why not go to college? After a long time I shaved in the morning. I even managed to take breakfast.

When I reached college everyone was surprised, including my lecturers. It was after a long time that I was attending first lecture. Bhusan asked me, "Have you taken any drug this morning that you made your way to college?"

"I think he has not taken any drug last night for a change, that's why he is here," Khan intervened.

"We really need to see in which direction has the sun risen from today." Even Prateesh got an opportunity to laugh.

"I think it's not Akash. It must be his twin. We need to do the DNA test. Then only he should be allowed in the class." Nishtha was ready with her expert opinion. I really didn't know how to answer them. Just then, the bell rang and I was saved from more humiliation.

It was Sridhar Sir's lecture. He was discussing the buying behaviour of consumers. It was some kind of model which is called as AIDA model. Sir was explaining, "A stand for Attention, I for Interest, D for Desire and A for Action." For another half an hour he explained how a marketer attracts the attention of consumer, creates interest for his product so that he/she has the desire to purchase which is reflected as action of buying. It was really interesting and I thought lectures were not so boring after all. Unlike B. Pharm, here there was more scope of learning and understanding, rather than just mugging. Close to ten minutes to end the class, Sir stopped to say,

"If you have any doubt then clear it now."

"Sir, can you tell us about some real cases related to this model?" It was Saikat. "Yes Saikat, tomorrow we will deal with case studies," Sir replied. "Any other doubt?"

"Sir I think this model is incomplete." I had the confusion.

"What you mean?"

"Sir I think it should be AIDAR model rather than AIDA model, where R stands for reaction, reaction of consumer. Once they have taken the action i.e. they have bought our product, we should know how they perceive our product, what they think about our product, how they rate our product. Simply speaking we should get the feed-back or reaction of the consumers, and then only the study of buying behaviour can be complete."

There was silence for few seconds. Then Sir spoke, "Actually you are correct Akash. No marketer can think or plan in vacuum. They should have the feedback. But this is an old model and we study it this way. Its improved version has not come yet. But you can postulate your own theory and who knows in coming years we might be reading Akash's model," sir said with a smile.

That moment was one of the defining moments of my M.Pharm due to two reasons: First, I realized that lectures aren't boring and there is ample opportunity to put your thoughts. This is what I wanted all through my B.Pharm. It was not necessary to follow the books blindly. I can have my own new ideas and it will be appreciated by our faculty members. Second thing that happened was, it changed the perception of my batchmates towards me. Well, they still treated me as an outcaste, but not because I was a master bunker, but because I could think differently which they couldn't do. They still considered me irresponsible and oh undisciplined guy, which no doubt I was but they realized that this guy was not a dumb or a fool.

When I came out of college, I saw Kislay and Simran waiting for me. Kislay said, "We were going to Santhala for tea. I thought you might be interested. Still there is time for lunch."

It seemed like that day was the day of surprises. First, Simran called to wake me up, then I found lectures interesting, and now Kislay was inviting me for tea when Simran was with him. Did this world change overnight!

"Kislay, you guys carry on. I will go to the hostel." I was still not sure whether Kislay really wanted me to come or it was just out of courtesy that he asked.

"What will you do in the hostel now? You can sleep in night. Come with us," Simran said almost with certain degree of authority, which only close friends possess.

"If I come, you both have to be ready for few litres of smoke." I smiled.

"Come on Akash, I am already used to it by now. Have you forgotten End Point sittings?" Kislay said mischievously.

"I am also getting used to it," Simran paused and said, "After yesterday." She started giggling again. My God how can someone be so happy all the time? We all walked to Santhala.

This time the waiter got us three cups of tea and one Wills Navy Cut without even bothering to ask. Thank God, no surprises here. Kislay started the conversation,

"It was nice concept Akash. Have you read it in some book before?"

"Not exactly the same thing, but I have been reading a few books of consumer behaviour. So just like that it came to my mind."

"Have we come here to discuss studies? Lectures and CL is enough I guess. Don't drag studies to the tea table at least." Simran was a bit irritated.

"That's fine Simran and by the way thanks for the wakeup call." I puffed the ciggie.

"In friendship, no sorry and no thanks!" Simran said leaning back. May be she was trying to save her lungs from passive smoking. "I know it's an old dialogue, but still it holds good for me."

"Point noted *yar*." This time I threw the smoke upwards in a pursuit of saving the lungs of my friends.

"Hey Kislay! We need to go to Udupi today in the evening. Remember or not?" Simran asked.

"Yes I remember. Akash why don't you join us?" Oh why was Kislay dragging me in all this, first tea, and now Udupi.

"Do you guys have any work there?"

"Actually Simran has to buy one handset." Kislay answered.

"One more? What happened to this one?" India is becoming richer I thought. Now people have more than one mobile. Who says India is a poor country.

"Actually I will have one post-paid connection. STD calls are very expensive on this network. I need a connection where I can talk unlimited on STD, at least night calls should be free." Simran's eyes lit up as she said those last words.

I was almost sure that it was a typical case of love. But I did not ask anything. I felt that I was still not close enough to her to intrude into her personal life. "Okay we will go in the evening." Although it meant missing my carom session, but I needed to return the favour of the wakeup call.

"5.30 pm will be fine," Kislay said. We finished our tea and moved to our respective hostels.

On our way to Udupi and during the sorting out process of handset, Simran herself told about her boyfriend, Raj whom she met three years back. He was then pursuing his MBA in Delhi. That time I understood why all of a sudden Kislay lost his interest in Simran. Obviously it was after this heart breaking news of Simran having a boy-friend. It took us about three hours to select the handset and network, which could match Simran's requirements. She was very much excited, "My day would start with Raj's Good Morning and end with his Good Night. The more I know him, the more I love him. He sometimes acts a bit indifferent, but most of the time he cares a lot about me. I really can't think of myself without him. He makes me feel so special, as if I am a princess." Simran spoke as if she was completely engrossed in love. A very dangerous sign indeed, because such type of love often leads to tormenting pain. I just wished Simran would never have to face such pain, as I know how it feels to be in that state.

Friendship Day

* * *

Days went flying by. It was month of August and Manipal was hit by monsoon. Weather in this month is much more pleasant and if it's not raining, the time is ideal for roaming out. By this time, Simran became my real buddy. It had become a routine for her to wake me up. I never had such a reliable alarm clock. I didn't know how and when she started taking care of all my needs. She would get me all the notes photocopied, remind me of the important topics from exam point of view, get me books that were necessary, and kept track of last date of assignments and project submissions. She even remembered whom I had lent money and when I was supposed to collect it. She made it mandatory for me to come to CL along with her and study subjects not only of my choice, but the one which were relevant from exam point of view also. It didn't mean that I didn't sit in the lobby anymore. I still did, but only to take breaks. From morning till the time CL was closed, we used to be together. We even joined BQ mess. Finally I had a friend, a girl with whom I could eat daily without getting bored. It was not like we only used to study. Simran was a fun loving girl, an all-time movie lover. We hardly missed out on any new releases. Every other evening, she would make some plans.

"Today we will go to the temple."

"Hey let's have *Litti* today in Pandey's Shop."

"Shall we go towards MIT today?"

"There is a sale in Udupi. We will go there."

"We will go to TC for sweet corn."

"After dinner we will have ice cream in Saiba."

"Spic Mackey is organized in Valley View. We will go there tonight."

We visited almost all the corners of Manipal and nearby places, except End Point. Simran had made up her mind that she would visit End Point only with Raj, whenever he would visit Manipal. I could never fathom why she wanted to do so. But then it was a matter of love, and when it is a matter of love, looking for a reason is unreasonable. Apart from that, Simran is very systematic in every aspect. She plans everything very well, when to study, when to go for a movie, when to eat non-veg, considering the days of week, when to study which subject, considering the dates of assignment, when to wear which colour dress again considering the days of week. I don't know why my batchmates labelled her as an idiot. But she was not so systematic all the time, especially when it came to movies. I still can't digest how she compelled me to go to Mangalore, which is two hours' drive from Manipal, just to watch *Rang De Basanti* in a multiplex. I consider myself to be a big movies fan, but even then in my B.Pharm, I never did this.

I still remember the day when I first met Simran, not knowing each other, not wanting to know, not even a smile back then! Then we started with a blank smile, then 'Hello', then it became 'Hey' which turned into '*Oye*' at last. We shared our days, hours, minutes and seconds. We made castles with our thoughts and moved mountains with our dreams. And today she is my best friend. I never ever thought that in M.Pharm I would have such a close friend with whom I could be as natural and as true as I used to be with my B.Pharm friends and now I don't find Manipal as boring as it used to be in first three months.

Kislay used to join us occasionally, but since he came to know about Simran's boyfriend, he totally lost interest in her. I don't think he was interested in friendship with Simran. He just wanted to date Simran and there was no more lust left in him. But Kislay used to have tea with me in hostel canteen and we still go to End Point occasionally. Whenever I was in the hostel, either I would be with Kislay or play carom. If I was outside, then most of the times I would be with Simran.

It was a Sunday and I was enjoying my late morning sleep, which had become a luxury for me off late, courtesy to Simran's wake up call. I heard my phone ring.

Knowing it's a Sunday, I ignored the call. But when it rang for the fourth time, I looked at my mobile. It was Simran.

"What the hell *yar*? Today is Sunday. Have you forgotten?" I was trying to figure out how Simran got it wrong.

"I have not forgotten Akash. I think you have forgotten." Simran took an unusually long pause.

"What have I forgotten? You know very well I really can't remember the last date of assignment submissions." I said thinking she might be talking about one of those assignments which we had to submit every second day in one subject or the other.

"You have become too studious, always thinking about assignments and deadlines." Simran giggled. By now I could understand the meaning behind her giggles. I was sure it wasn't about assignments. But instead of being relieved, I was more aghast now. Who knows she might have planned yet another tour of Mangalore or any other such thing. This Simran can do anything.

"Then what's the matter? Tell me."

"Today is first Sunday of August. Happy Friendship Day Akash."

"Oh yes! I totally forgot. Happy Friendship Day *yar*. Any plans?"

"Nothing much. We will meet for dinner. I just called to wish you. I wanted my best friend to be the person whom I wished first."

"Ok Simran. See you at dinner. Bye for now."

On Sundays, we used to be in our respective hostels. She utilizes her Sunday talking to Raj and me playing carom. Both happy in the company of their beloveds, although carom is not my first love. Obviously it is Neelu and the mark she has left, God knows, will that ever be erased or not.

I got up from my bed thinking of Friendship Day. For all, love victimized hearts there are two days which are of utmost importance, one is Valentine's Day and the other is Friendship Day. For the youth in college, these days are like a mega festival, which celebrated like Holi and Diwali and my case was no different. But unfortunately, I could never celebrate Valentine's Day with Neelu, but I did celebrate Friendship Day once with her. So for me Friendship Day is much more important than Valentine's Day.

I don't need to have a sharp memory to remember that first and last Friendship Day which I celebrated with Neelu. No guy could ever forget first date, first hug, first kiss, first love letter, first ride on bike, and of course first Valentine's Day and Friendship day. I can't say that she was my girlfriend back then. We were not like regular couple. Anything related to Neelu was never normal and usual. But we were very close to each other, at least I felt so. It was during this period that it became a routine for me to call her at 10.30 pm daily. I would call her in the room, as she didn't have a mobile. It was like a rule for me to call her, whatever might happen, even Neelu made it mandatory, by default to be in her room at that particular time. Wherever she was, whatever she is doing, no matter what her condition was, she used to be near the phone at 10.30. One day I realized her desperateness to be in room waiting for the call when she answered phone after two full rings, breathing heavily like a 100 meter sprinter. Obviously out of concern I asked her, "Hey Neelu, what's wrong? Why are you panting so heavily?"

"No, nothing. Just like that." That was Neelu, who never answers anything in the first go. You need to ask her again and again, which I ultimately did.

"What you mean by just like that? You are panting so hard. It seems you have been running. Tell me what's happening there. I need to know." There was a pause. That's what she does. If she doesn't want to speak about something, she will just press her mute button on. "Okay. Look Neelu I am getting worried now. Tell me what's the matter?" I again forced her to speak.

"Akash I am telling you there is nothing to be worried. I am fine." She was still wheezing.

"I know there is something wrong or else you can't be so breathless. But let it be. If you don't want to tell, it's fine. You need not tell me everything happening around you." That was an EB. I knew it will work.

"Oh Akash, you know very well there is nothing I can't tell you." Neelu said it with such innocence that only she could manage. It's this innocence of her voice, which made me crazy about her.

"But you will laugh a lot." This time she mocked her voice like a baby. Yet another quality to drive me crazy.

"Why would I laugh? Come on dear, now don't create Ramsey brothers movie's suspense." "Actually, since evening I was in Anu's room." Neelu took a pause which was too long, which clearly meant that I have to pin her again to speak. "She is your batchmate, good friend and you two are in the same hostel. What's the big deal if you were in her room?" I was still trying to figure out the relation between Neelu's panting and her presence in Anu's room since evening.

"No actually we two were so engrossed in a chit chat that I did not notice the time. When I saw the time, it was already 10.30. So I walked briskly to my room all the way from ground floor." As a matter of fact Neelu's room was on the fifth floor and I knew her brisk walking meant half walking and half running. I have seen her do that on her way to college, whenever she was late.

"Oh." I was wondering what excuse Neelu might have given to Anu for her sudden departure. She can't reveal the true reason, for sure.

"To make the matters worse, when I reached near the corridor, I heard the phone ringing in my room. I knew it was you. So I ran to my room, which is at the end of the corridor. Somehow I opened the lock just in time to receive your call, when it rang again." I could feel that desperation to pick the phone in her voice.

"Take it light dear. A delay of five or ten minutes won't kill me." I laughed, but deep inside I was outrageously happy to know the importance of this 10.30 call in Neelu's life. Yet another factor to make me crazier for her.

She used to share everything with me. Even about her parents and family. "You know Akash, my dad is having backache again. I am asking him to take a leave, but he is such a workaholic."

"My mom cooked *Padambari* today. It's a typical Malayalam recipe. I will learn when I go home this time. I need to learn cooking."

"My uncle is coming from Saudi. I hope I get some nice chocolates."

"Can you believe Akash my sister is having an affair and that too with a North Indian guy."

It could be about her room.

"Akash, I am sitting on a table. I am so scared to put my feet down. I saw two cockroaches. One of them was flying."

"My fan makes too much sound. I think I should complain."

"You know my *Akka* is pregnant. So I don't let her clean my room. I do it myself and just sign in her register that she has cleaned" or could be about her batchmates as well.

"Akash, Anoop topped again in the sessional. But this guy is some creature. You know today in the lab he was telling me the story of *Panchtantra*."

"Akash, have you seen that see-saw in the park near the temple. Anu and I played on that see-saw today evening."

"I think Kunal is taking drugs. His eyes are bloody red all the time."

"You know I think Varneeta has a soft corner for you. Today she almost fought with the class , defending the point that you are the best director of our college."

It could be about the lectures and practical.

"Today Shaunbag Sir took the first lecture.

He told that he would not only teach the subject, but also how to write it in exams and score maximum marks."

"You are so lucky. You don't have to face Chaudhary Sir till you are in the third year. He makes life pathetic in Med Chem lab. No doubt he is nick named as *Sher Khan*. Today he shouted at me for no fault of mine. He said if I continue carrying out my practical like this, it would be better to either jump out of this window or he himself would jump out of it, or even better if we both jump out of this window together. Even I could not hold my temper and replied politely that this window is too small for both of us to jump together and I am in no mood of committing suicide. So it will be better, if you jump out of this window alone."

"Pharmacognosy is too tough. I can't remember the names of so many drugs. Tell me some way out."

She used to give a report of the full day's happenings. She once said, "If I don't share anything with you, it seems like the incidence has not happened at all. If I don't speak my heart out, I can't sleep."

We used to talk for hours over the phone. Sometimes till 4 am in the morning. That was one more reason for me to bunk the morning classes. I am still amazed how Neelu managed to come to college at 8 am looking all fresh and energetic, whereas it was difficult for me to attend even 11 o' clock lectures. Nevertheless we followed this 10.30 rule for quite some time. This golden phase continued for about eight months. It was during this phase that Friendship Day came. I still remember that day, as if it had happened just yesterday. Neelu's exams were over and it was vacation time for her. But she stayed back as she was the editor of the college magazine and she had to finish the magazine work. I had preparatory leave for my university exams which were about to start in just three days.

I remember she came at 10.15 am, although the meeting time was 10.00 am. It was her habit of always coming late by 15-20 minutes, but even then I always used to be on time. Once she herself said, "You know very well I never come on time. No matter how much I try, I always get late. Then why the hell you keep coming on time?"

"You know Neel, I have never understood the meaning of the line, *Intejar ka bhi apna maja hai(waiting has its own pleasures)*. Now I know how it feels like. I am just enjoying my waiting time. It is fun. Hope someday you would also have that fun." I used to call her Neel whenever I felt romantic.

I was waiting on the stairs of the Physiology department, which is just adjacent to LH. It was a Sunday and I knew no one would come to that side. Romance is much better in a deserted arena. But it's impossible to find such a place in Manipal. So I choose the place which was closest to be deserted. I was in a doubt, whether Neelu would agree to come there. I could never be sure about this girl's thinking process. But I was amazingly pleased when she agreed.

I saw her coming. She was wearing a black suit which I had never seen before. May be it was kept for this special occasion. She was also wearing a pearl necklace tightly embracing her neck. That was surprising too, as Neelu was never fond of ornaments. She kept her hair open, which were half-wet because of the shower she might have taken just before coming here. I always loved her hair left loose, but for some strange reason Neelu was very reluctant to keep her them open. With every passing second, she looked more beautiful, more lovable than ever before. When she was just couple of paces away, the air got filled with the aroma of Mogra, the scent which she never applied again. I also noticed two small pimples on her nose that made her even cuter. I felt as if a fairy walked right into my heart. I had never seen Neelu in that attire before. I did not blink even for a second. I could not have missed even a single second of this Neelu. I could have stared even longer, but then Neelu came and said, "You donkey, why were you dying to meet? You have exams in just three days. You should not be wasting time *yar*."

I wanted to say, 'I can fail in all my exams if you keep showing me this avatar of yours'. But I had to talk sensibly and responsibly, "I know Neelu exams are very near. That's why I asked to meet just for half an hour."

"A very Happy Friendship Day Akash." Neelu shook hands with me. I was in no mood of letting that hand go.

"Wish you same." Neelu sat beside me on the stairs. Her hands were still in mine and she made no efforts to remove it. We were sitting really close, as if for the first time she didn't care who was watching, who might comment, what her friends would think. Every now and then I could feel the warmth of her breath which I felt sometimes on my cheek and sometimes on my hair. We sat like that without speaking anything. It was a divine feeling and even a guy like me didn't have any words to justify those moments. It was Neelu who spoke first, "Akash." Again, there was a pause, which meant I needed to speak. Slowly I looked into her eyes. She was not even looking at me. She was avoiding eye contact. May be she was shy.

"Yes Neel."

"I forgot *yar*. I have got this chocolate for you." She opened her left hand and gave me the chocolate. There was something written in Arabic on that chocolate, which means it's one of those imported Saudi Chocolates. Chocolate had melted completely, so tightly she was holding it. May be she was nervous.

Just then I remembered that even I bought few gifts for her. I was coming back to my senses. I took out the friendship band from my pocket.

"I know I am not SRK, but you are for sure Rani Mukherjee, every guy wants to be with you."

"Shut up Akash. You are such a donkey." By now I knew that whenever she called me donkey, she wanted to show her closeness towards me. I again took her hands in mine and started tying the band on her wrist.

"Akash I always wish, you could have been in my batch. I could have met you so much more freely." With those words she laid her head on my shoulder. I could not believe, was it really happening or I am just dreaming? I felt like pinching myself, as seen in the movies. Time flew away. Time is the most elastic element in this world, it increases the minutes when we are waiting and decreases the hours when we are enjoying.

"Akash look at the time. It's 1 o' clock. You don't want to study or what!" Neelu was almost shouting.

"I should not have come. I should not have disturbed you during your exam period. When there were my University exams, we hardly talked. And when it's your exam, I wasted so much time of yours."

'Oh God!' I was almost pleading; 'don't make Neelu feel guilty'. It was true that we didn't talk during her exams. Reason was obvious, marks did matter to her. She was among the top five students in her batch, a distinction holder. But for me marks were at the bottom of the priority.

"You donkey, not even a minute more here. Go to your mess now, have food, take a small nap of not more than fifteen minutes and then start studying." Neelu was in no mood to sit there. All the romance had vanished.

"Okay Neelu, I am leaving. But..."This time I took a pause.

"But what, Akash?"Neelu looked directly into my eyes, trying to read my expressions and trying to reveal the mystery of my pause. She guessed that my master stroke is going to come, which I saved for the last minute.

I just smiled, winked my eyes and took out the card from inside of my shirt,

"Happy Friendship Day, my Neel." Neelu eye's popped out, "Oh, why didn't you give it till now? Some kind of surprise? Let me see inside this. I am sure there must be one of your poems." She was correct. Now I do write customized poems for her. Our closeness was enough for me to write poems for her.

"Now will I have to beg you to narrate the poem? You know my Hindi is not so good, although I have done my schooling in KV." Every now and then Neelu had this nag of talking about her school, *Kendriya Vidhayalaya*. I narrated the poem and Neelu was spell bound listening to those lines...

Ajnabi khamosi teri jane kya kah gayi! Najro ki haya jane kya bayan kar gayi! Uthti girti palko ki angraiya, Dil ko jane kyo dharka gayi.

Sharmati muskan teri jane kya kah gayi, Alsai angrai teri jane kya bayan kar gayi, Soti-jagti aankhon ki gahraiya, Dil ko jane kyo dharka gayi.

Ajnabi khamosi teri jane kya kah gayi! Najro ki haya jane kya bayan kar gayi!

"Is this written for me? I can't believe it. I am feeling as if I am flying high in the air, that too without any drug." Neelu came alarmingly close to me and in a fraction of second, happened the impossible. Neelu kissed on my lips and in no time we were smooching. I felt lightning, thundering all around me. I felt my head spinning like a top. That's the best gift I could ever get on Friendship Day. It took me a while to get back to normal. When I came to my usual self, I saw Neelu standing.

"Akash I am going to hostel now or else the mess will close. You also go and study and don't think you are going to get that again." I did not know she meant it seriously. It remained my first and last kiss.

I also walked to my mess. All the time I was reliving that kiss. I was wondering if that was a momentary emotional outburst or Neelu had planned that before. I thought, I knew the reason why she accepted to come to Physiology department. Needless to say, rest of the day I could not study even a single word. Every time I tried to concentrate, I felt Neelu's presence around. Neelu was simply magical. She was addictive, her voice, her talking style, her gait were all very addictive. There was a faith in her smile, an invitation in her eyes. Her personality was like a rainbow, full of colours. She was the princess of her magical state.

Koi kahe, Kahta rahe kitna bhi humko diwana,my cell was ringing. I came back to my present world from the memories of sweetest Friendship Day of my life. It was Simran on line, "Hey Akash, just called to check what you are doing? I guess you have slept again, as you did not reply to my SMS."

"Ya Simran, I dozed off again. After all its Sunday." I could not say that I was dreaming with open eyes for last few hours.

"Ok. Now get up and go to the mess. It's already 1.30. I am also going to LH mess with my roommate." I washed my face and went to the mess. I was wondering what would have happened to me, if this girl Simran would not have come to Manipal. At least now I have some discipline in my life. She provided the steering which was missing all through my UG days.

Sessional Exams

* * *

It was the month of September, the month of havoc for all of us. First sessional exams were scheduled from 10th of this month. This was the first experience of new students at the college, of back-to-back examinations, which happens in Manipal only. No doubt my batch mates were horrified. All of them were having their own methods to combat this 'back to back' venture. Almost all of them were sitting in the lobby of CL and sharing their views about this forthcoming tornado.

Saikat said, "If we can do the syllabus at least once we can write in exams pretty well. I am confident that if I am thorough with the portion, I can write well in exams."

"Thorough with the portion! You must be kidding. It's impossible to read them even once, forget about being thorough." That was Bhusan.

"I always believe in discussing. That has worked for me always. So I will just be discussing all the topics with Khan. Even when we are in our respective hostels, we will discuss over phone," Nishtha said and Khan nodded.

"I think I will just study the notes. There is no point reading these fat books. On the day of exam, you won't be able to recall so many things. So why to waste time in reading the books." Darshan's idea was not bad at all.

"Whatever you do, it all boils down to the night before exam." Kislay spoke and all went silent. They knew Kislay has been giving these back-to-back exams for last four years. Kislay continued, "If you can revise the whole syllabus even once before the night of exam, it will be enough."

"That's not a big deal. I study all the topics, same day when they are dealt in class. So it won't be difficult for me." Shweta sounded confident enough.

"For first two papers it won't be much difficult. However, after third paper your mind just gets fatigued. You cannot pull all nighters for seven continuous exams. Moreover, if you don't revise it before the day of exam, whatever you have studied is all waste. Therefore, as I said, it just boils down to the night before exam. If you have the stamina to study for the entire night, without letting your brain efficiency drain out, back to back papers won't be so difficult for you." Kislay's last line made my classmates even more horrified.

I was also sitting there. But no one cared about my opinion. They were in no mood of hearing my philosophy of marks being insignificant. I was no doubt more regular in college, but still my perception about marks had not changed. Just then Prateesh unnecessarily dragged me into the conversation, "Akash, you have been doing so well in practicals. I know GD and debates are your forte. Assignments also you manage pretty well. But how do you think, you will cope up with the theory papers?"

I was about to speak, just then Nishtha opened her

big fat mouth, "Oh Prateesh, why are you bringing the laziest living creature into all this. Akash is more than happy with his practical marks. He never expected to score that much. Why would he bother to lead sleepless nights just for some fucking extra marks? Let this lazy guy sleep with mental peace." Everyone was looking at each other's face. Nishtha's comments were too harsh and it was evident from my facial expressions that I did not like it, not even a single bit. Khan tried to sooth me, "Akash, what she meant to say is that..."

"Khan, Nishtha is absolutely correct. I am lazy and that's a proven fact. I have never denied that. But I just want to say one thing." I took a pause. After a long time I decided not to ignore. Enough is enough.

"Progress is not made by early risers or hard workers, but by lazy people trying to find the easier way to do the same thing. I think Nishtha is intelligent enough to understand, what I mean." There was complete silence for few seconds, as if I have slapped Nishtha. There was no point in me staying there anymore. I came out of the CL and called Simran, "Hi Simran. Are you done with your beautification in parlour or not?"

"What happened Akash? You seem to be upset." Simran could easily understand my mood.

"Nothing *yar*. Just this *moti* Nishtha. God knows what she thinks of herself." I narrated the whole episode in short.

"Ok Akash. Just take a chill pill. How many times have I said to you, not to lose your temper. Anyway I am still in the parlour. See you at dinner."

"Ok Simran. See ya." I went to LP to have my dose of tea and ciggie, till dinner time.

Over dinner my mood was no better and surprisingly Simran was also silent.

Simran spoke for the first time "Tell me Akash, why did you feel so bad?"

"I don't know." I put my hands up in the air.

"Akash you know what your problem is? You cannot accept the truth." Simran was looking directly into my eyes. There was something in those eyes that made me immediately look down to my plate.

"You always say marks don't bother you. But if that's the case then why were you so ecstatic when you topped in the GD for the first time? Why the hell were you on cloud nine when we two got second highest marks in debate? You were so happy that you even missed your carom session that day, that too for some stupid chit chat. Even after that whenever you got good marks in practicals, you were overjoyed. So don't give out statements that marks never bothered you." It was first time, Simran was speaking like this. I had never ever imagined she could be so rude. As a matter of fact, truth is always brutal and sounds rude.

"Deep inside you, there is the living desire of getting good marks. But you know very well that your laziness, indiscipline and erratic life style would never let you do so. That's why you always try to cover up your weakness by not giving a damn about marks and the grade system. Why don't you accept the truth that you would love to have good marks, but you are not capable enough of doing that?" Simran's face was almost red after that staggering and shattering speech. I pushed my plate away. "Simran I am not used to people talking to me in loud voice and nobody ever taught me about my life style and my *fundas* of life. You too better not do that." I got up and moved out of mess without even bothering to look at Simran's reaction or what she was trying to speak.

I went directly to LP, ordered tea and ciggie. I needed ciggie badly to sooth myself and to think over what had just happened. Was Simran correct? Did I really care about my marks? Did marks really bother me? Was I really lazy enough not to score good marks and that's why I use some pretext or other? There was no doubt that I was happy when I topped in GD and even after that whenever I surpassed Nishtha in marks, I was happy. So, to some extent Simran was correct. Marks did bother me and yes, with all my laziness I would never be able to score good marks in theory papers.

I kept analysing the things for about an hour or so and at the end I thought I unfolded yet another mystery of human psychology. A true friend always does two things in extremes, one is silently caring and other is openly hurting, just to make you perfect. Simran had been doing the first thing since we became friends and just now she has done the second thing. I realized that Simran did hurt me, but it was for my benefit, just to make me understand myself and what I did? I left her alone in the mess. I didn't even listen to her or looked back at her.

I should call her now.

"Simran, can we meet now? Please. I am waiting outside CL." I was almost pleading.

"It's already late *yar*. We will meet tomorrow in college." Simran sounded very low.

"It's only 11. Still one hour before the closing time of hostel. Come *na*." I pleaded.

"Ok. I am coming."

Simran came within five minutes. "Simran I am sorry for my behaviour in the mess."

"Oh is it? Anything else you want to say Mr. Akash?" Simran folded her hands, which meant she did not really like the conversation. I was thinking what to say next. Just then Simran spoke, "You always say that you don't forget things easily. But I don't think so."

I was preparing myself for yet another lecture, wondering what wrong I did again!

"Don't you remember my *funda* of life, in friendship no sorry, no thanks?" And Simran giggled. I can't say how much I liked that giggle. At last Simran was smiling.

"Akash, I know I have…" I interrupted her in between.

"Simran please don't say anything. I understood what you meant. You were correct. I cannot bust my ass studying all the time. That's not me! You may call it my laziness and yes I do love to get good marks.

Who wouldn't be happy to stand apart in crowd? I have always done that in extra-curricular activities, but never in studies. I really enjoyed it when I topped in class. But Simran, the fact also remains that I cannot study beyond a limit."

"I have never asked you to study all the time. But Akash think; in UG you led the life you wanted. Why don't you try to change it in PG? Just for one year try to lead a life which your parents are expecting, which your teachers are expecting, which your real well wishers are expecting. There is no harm in trying. If you don't like it, you always have the option of reverting to your previous lifestyle."

"Simran I have already changed my ways." I was still unsure, what she was expecting from me.

"Yes you have. But why don't you give your cent percent? And remember what you said to Nishtha today. Don't you want to prove yourself right, Akash?" Simran touched my Achilles heel.

"Oh actually that line was said by Mr. Henry Ford in one of his interviews. Those were not my words." I was kind of backing off.

"Akash it was you who said it in front of our class. Now you have to show your progress, either by finding an easier way or by hard work, it doesn't matter. You just have to do it. You cannot back off now."

"Simran it's easy to say than actually doing it. You know very well that there is no easier way of getting good marks. It's just hard work."

"Then do it *na!* There is no problem in trying at least." Simran was best at convincing. She could convince for any damn thing.

"But there are only ten days left for sessional exams." I was still not sure how would I justify my big words that I had said in front of all.

"Ten days are enough. In your B.Pharm days, you used to start preparing for exams seven days before the date of exam, one day for each subject. Right?" Simran questioned as if she is taking my viva.

"Ya, right."

"And you never used to study anything before that. You didn't even bother to open books one week before exam, right?" Simran asked in the same tone.

"Ya, right." I again replied like an obedient student.

"And in spite of all that you managed to score about seventy percent, right?" Simran's tone was a bit softer this time.

"Ya, right."

"Now in this sessional you have ten days time. It means about one and a half day for each subject, about fifty percent more time for each subject compared to your UG days. And you have already studied a lot of things. At least for last two months you have been studying more or less about the subject matter, which you never did in your UG days. It means if you are ready to bust your ass, you can surely get good marks." Simran explained the things in a crystal clear manner. She has this unique ability to convince people by her logics and reasoning. Once again I had no choice, but to agree.

"Simran, I think you are correct. At least I can try. For once let me lead a life which my parents would ideally expect from me and let me work." I felt a unique energy, a unique strength inside me. May be it was because of that the thoughts of my parents.

"Akash it's 12. Let me go in now. And yes you can bunk college from tomorrow. Just be in your room and study. If there is anything important in class I will let you know. Good night *yar*." Simran went inside her hostel and I also walked towards my hostel.

Next morning my routine changed. I had only one thing left to do, study and more study. I left taking lunch or dinner, as full stomach made me sleepy and lazy. I would have cup noodles, which were available just outside my hostel. That was the only solid food I used to take. Apart from that it was all liquid and gas. I even left bathing and shaving just to save time. I also switched off my mobile, so that there was no disturbance. I never slept for more than fifteen minutes at a stretch. This nap of fifteen minutes I used to take about eight to ten times in twenty four hours. It was my power nap and I felt being reenergized soon after that nap. It is needless to say that my ciggie consumption increased to an alarming level. It was my only ammunition to combat sleep. I even tried *gutkha* to keep myself awake. There was only one problem. Whenever I used to sit on my chair I would feel sleepy. Only way to overcome that was to walk and study. Sometimes I used to walk in my room, but room being too small didn't offer a good roaming area. So I decided to use my hostel corridor. For hours I used to walk from one end of the corridor to the other with book in one hand and ciggie in other. Sometimes ciggie was replaced by cup noodles. I did everything possible to finish syllabus twice before exams and I succeeded doing that to a large extent. I left no stone unturned. At last the exams started.

After a long time I met my friends, including Simran. Simran looked surprised, "Look at you Akash! You are looking like a dacoit with your beard and your eyes, so red. You seem to have lost weight too. You look sick. Are you okay?"

"Simran I am fine. It's just that I have not shaved, nothing else."

"You know Akash, Prateesh and Bhusan were saying to some other guys that you have gone mad." Simran giggled. I understood the meaning of that giggle. It was not a carefree giggle, it was a nervous giggle.

"They were saying that whenever they come out of their room, whether it is in the afternoon or early morning or at midnight, they see you in the corridor roaming up and down with a ciggie in your hand. They were even saying that you have not slept for the last seven days or so."

"Simran, no human being can live without sleeping. Don't worry. It's nothing like that. And now let's go inside the exam hall." I was in no mood of listening or discussing about what people think of me.

"Ok Akash. All the best!" "Good luck to you too, Simran."

Soon all the seven papers were over. I knew I had done pretty well. I was just waiting for the results with my fingers crossed. Simran was also pretty confident. So were Nishtha and Khan. First time in Manipal I was feeling enthusiastic to know my sessional marks. Finally, the marks were displayed on the notice board. My name was at the top of the list. Yes, I had topped! Nishtha was second, followed by Saikat, Simran and Khan. I felt as if I had achieved something substantial for the first time. I had cleared entrance of UG and then PG, but those were because of my luck and to some extent due to my intelligence. There was no hard work involved in that. Here whatever I have achieved was because of my sheer hard work. My friends barring Nishtha and Khan took the results quite sportingly. They were somehow expecting this after seeing my horrendous study cycle before exams. Anyway, I proved my point and I was least bothered who was thinking what! There were only two people who were genuinely happy. One was obviously Simran and other was Manthan Sir. After all, his student was doing justice to his potentials!

Time flows at a brisk pace in Manipal, especially when you have happening friends and fun loving group. I didn't have a group, but I had a happening friend. In addition to that I was giving a lot of time to my studies. I had to finish assignments, do projects, prepare for GD and debates and of course attended all the theory classes and even extra classes. A guy like me who always believed in hitting fours and sixes in slog overs was accumulating ones and twos. So time flew even more quickly. I balanced my life pretty well between fun activities and studies, or I should say Simran made me balance my life between studies and fun activities. We visited all the nearby tourist places like Kudremukh, Kasargaud, Jog falls and Murdeshwara. Visiting the beaches of Malpe and Kaup was a weekly activity. Sometimes Kislay and other batch mates accompanied us as well. After the sessional marks we two were not an outcaste any more. Soon it was time for second sessional and I was back to my rigorous routine of exam period. It meant I slept as less as possible, walked through the corridor day and night, had about fifteen cup noodles daily and lost the count of my ciggie. But result was not as overwhelming as it was in the first sessional. This time Nishtha topped, me being second.

Utsav Time

* * *

Soon after the sessionals it was the time for fun. It was the time of Utsav, the inter college cultural competition. That's the only time when I enjoy college most and all through my B.Pharm, I had never ever bunked college during that period! Actually Utsav is a three day gala, but its preparation starts about a month prior. All twenty seven colleges of Manipal University try their best to win the overall champions trophy. It's a matter of pride for any Dean or Principal to hold the overall winner's trophy. That's the only time when the Hitler type professors smile at me and talk softly, rather than bashing me or tormenting at me. The reason was obvious. All hefty cruel professors knew that with Akash around its sure that all acting events prizes will be bagged by our college, MCOPS, be it in mimes, skits or mad ads. Even prizes in solo events like JAM and extempore was almost sure. So I was kind of star of my college and I was given a treatment, a star deserve. Don't think that there were guys or girls waiting for my autograph! It happens with movie stars only, not in college. Only star treatment I got was, I was allowed to bunk classes and was marked present by my professors. Actually that was more than enough for me. Attendance of one whole month without attending even a single lecture, was as good as winning an Oscar for me.

The moment the dates of Utsav were announced, there was a hullaballoo in the college. For a jiffy, even the professors decided to give studies a break and for a change they were discussing Utsav among themselves. Busiest were the cultural secretary of the college, a very nice and immensely talented guy from B.Pharm, third year. This guy Shashank is a one man army when it comes to music. He can play guitar, mandolin, key board, mouth organ, *tabla* and each one with same proficiency. He was running here and there, sometimes to the principal's cabin, sometimes to cultural-in-charge Prof Mallikarjun, at times to the finance department and sometimes to his other cultural team members.

"Hey Akash." It was Simran. "College seems to be fully engrossed in Utsav mood. I am so excited. I have heard so much about it from you guys. I am eagerly waiting for it. I want to eat in those food stall, want to see those amazing dances live whose video I have seen, want to see that Rangoli competition, that bold and hot fashion show and of course want to see my best friend performing." She was speaking non-stop. By now I was used to it.

"Yes Simran. It would be a good experience. Nice break from studies."

"Hey Akash Sir." Shashank came yelling from a distance. It's customary in our college to address seniors by Sir.

"Yes Shashank, you look very busy. Relax *yar*, you have one month's time." I said smiling. I know how tough it is to be the cultural secretary. There are thousand things he had to look after and expectations were always very high. Cultural secretary of all the colleges leave no stone unturned to win and Sanky was no exception. "Sir, have you checked the schedule of events? Oh, it's still not displayed on the notice board. How can you see! That's why I came searching for you." He seems to be totally confused and understandably so. After all he was under the pressure of leading the college in Utsav.

"Sir, this time two acting events are on the same day. Skit is in the afternoon of the second day and mimes in the evening, same day. Sir, you have to manage somehow."

"Sanky I am getting old dear. I don't think I can handle so many things this time." I smiled, took a pause and continued. "In fact I don't think I can participate in any event. DP is good. He can handle the things well. You let him handle the acting events."

Shashank had an expression as if someone had given a full blow on his chest. He was almost holding his breath. More than expression of surprise, he had an expression of horror. Even Simran's expressions were no better.

"Sir, what are you saying? We cannot even imagine competing in acting events without you. You know these KMC guys. They are damn good. Each year they come up with some new idea. DP won't be able to handle it all alone. We need you Sir."

"No one is mandatory Sanky. Life goes on. Our college will win, with me or even without me. I think you have forgotten that last year I had said that I am retiring from competitive field. I might do it for fun, not for any competition."

"Sir, I thought that 15x3 i.e. 45 points are sure shot in acting events. If you back out like this I will be in a big mess." Sanky's looks were that of pleading. The only option he could find was to drag Simran in this, "Ma'am, you please try to convince Akash Sir. I never expected that there will be an acting event and he will not participate."

"Akash, I think Shashank is right." Simran who was quite all the while started to speak, "As far as I know you, acting is your hobby. In fact it's not your hobby, it's your passion! How can you deny participating, that to when it's the matter of your alma mater! Don't you want your college to win the trophy?"

"Simran, it's always good to quit when you are on top. Last year we bagged the first prize in all the three acting events. You know skit is my favourite event, but till last year we could never manage to get first position in that. Once we got first prize in that along with mimes and mad ads I decided it's time to retire."

"Come on Akash you are speaking as if you are Guru Dutt or James Cameroon, who has won academy-awards. And even they didn't retire after winning Oscars.

Have you gone crazy? It's just a college competition." Simran could not justify my logic of not participating and the anger was apparent in her voice.

"Sir, you are the best director of Manipal. We all know it. If you lose a few events here and there, it will not make you any less talented person. Sir you please go to Santhala, have a ciggie and think over it. However I will come to your room at night."

After fifteen minutes I was sitting in Santhala along with Simran, sipping tea and smoking ciggie. Simran was still mad at me and was almost screaming, "Akash I always knew that you are a psycho. You have your own weird reasoning for all the things, but this one is unbelievable. I mean how can you even think like this. Is this another attention seeking effort of yours? What are you up to? What do you want? All the people cajole you to participate, so that you feel you are the important one and wanted?

Is that what you want?"

"Damn it Simran! I don't want that and I am going." I was about to get up.

"Don't you dare go leaving me sitting here like this? You have done it once. Don't repeat the same mistake again." Simran was commanding me. That's the tone I always hate. But I knew one thing. It's okay to commit a mistake. Each time you commit a new mistake you learn a new thing, which in turn leads to your growth as a person. But if you commit same mistake again, it's no more a mistake. It's a sin. I decided not to increase my already alarmingly high level of sins committed. I sat down quietly. After a pause of two minutes Simran spoke again in a very soft and mellowed tone, "What's the matter Akash? Tell me *na*." She looked directly in my eyes. I hate when she does that, because I can't lie then.

"You know Simran, acting is a team event. Everyone thinks Akash is the best director. It's not like that. Akash is the best only because of his team. Without my team I cannot do anything."

"You cannot do anything or you don't want to do anything?"

"I don't know, may be both. I don't want to perform on that stage without my core team. Last year it was so difficult to do it without Neelu and Surojit *da*. You know I met Neelu first time during our skit in the first year. I knew her closely as a person because of these acting events and we also came close during those events only. It was this stage which made Neelu a part of my life and without Neelu I don't feel like making this stage a part of my life. It's impossible to perform without Neelu, in my team." Surojit *da* was Neelu's batchmate.

"So it's because Neelu is not here, you are not performing?"

"No Simran. It's not only about Neelu. You know, it was Surojit *da* who actually made me realize my potentials. It was he, who had asked me to direct the skit when I was in the first year. It was a big thing to allow the most junior person to direct a skit and you know my batchmates Vicky, Aditya, Shelly, Surya, Anshuk, Megha, Pallavi, they never questioned me. What I am doing, why I am doing. They believed in me, right from the script writing to dialogue delivery. If I am known today in Manipal, it's all because of those guys, who made me the best director. I owe these people a lot and I don't want to perform without them."

"And what about your juniors like DP and Shashank? Are they not part of your team? Won't they feel bad?"

"Yes they will. And I know Sanky and DP are not going to spare me so easily.

But..." I gestured the waiter to get me one

"Enough Akash! You have already smoked four. You don't care about your lungs, please care for mine" That same mesmerizing innocence came on her face again. It was almost impossible to ignore her when she spoke so cutely. The only problem was that she seldom did so.

"Okay I am not smoking, but can I have tea?"

"So you have decided finally that you will not participate?"

"Ya, pretty much decided."

"And you think Shashank and DP will not pressurize you?"

"I have to convince them somehow." Just then my mobile rang.

"Simran someone is calling from college's landline number." I was totally surprised. Generally call comes from college's office when you are in the defaulter's list due to some reason. I started to think of any disciplinary issue or attendance issue.

"Will you pick the damn call?" Simran shouted again.

"Is it Akash speaking?" A deep heavy husky South Indian voice echoed in my ears.

I have heard this voice, but could not recognise it at that moment.

"Yes! Akash speaking." I was suspicious.

"This is Mallikarjun. I want to meet you now. Come to college." He didn't even bother to ask where I am, what am I doing, but that's Dr. Mallikarjun for you, the professor I dreaded most.

"Simran what the hell is this? Why does Mallik sir want to meet me?"

"Relax Akash. It must be related to Utsav. He is cultural-in-charge after all."

Simran tried to console me. I paid the bill and we started walking towards college. I was sweating profusely.

"Why are you so worried? Mallik sir has called you just to talk. He is not going to kill you." Simran was trying her best to ease me.

"You don't know Mallik sir properly as you have never attended his lectures. You know once in Viva, I gave one wrong answer and guess what he said! He said, "Shit man, you should be sent to jail." Which teacher can send you to jail for the offence of giving one wrong reply in viva! You don't know Mallik Sir properly."

"Akash I know this incidence. You have already told me. That happened when you were in second year B.Pharm, almost four years back. Time has changed since then. Now you are a post graduate student." Simran was trying to give me some mental strength.

"Nothing changes with Mallik Sir. You forgot the incidence that happened just four months back?"

"Which incidence?" Simran looked puzzled. "Oh you don't know. I was standing outside our department in the corridor looking at the notice board. Mallik Sir walked passed me. Then all of a sudden he came back and started shouting in his full voice. 'Hey you are Akash, right? You don't have any work to do? Always wasting your time here and there? Why don't you do anything productive?' Cheeh man!"

"Why did he say like that? We don't even have to study his subject in M.Pharm?" Simran asked.

"Same question was haunting my mind. What the hell have I done to piss him off! His voice was so loud that other professors and lab attendants came out. Even the sweeper who doesn't understand even a single word of Hindi or English was enjoying the show."

"So a full scene was created. How did I miss that? I would have loved to see you in that state." Simran giggled. "But what was the reason of all that scolding? Did you come to know?"

"Yes I came to know after two three minutes, when he said you had attendance shortage in B.Pharm and still you are bunking classes in M.Pharm. Cheeh man! Lecture is going on and you are standing here? Don't you have any shame?" I continued after swallowing the lump in my throat. "When I peeped inside the classroom I saw that Pharmacology lecture was on. I said very gently to Mallik Sir that I am pursuing my M.Pharm in Pharma Management and not Pharmacology."

"Oh my God! I can't believe it. You were scolded for not attending the lecture which you were never supposed to attend?" Simran was laughing with her full throttle. "But what was Mallik Sir's reaction after knowing that he has scolded you for no reason. Did he say sorry or something like that?"

"Sorry??? You must be kidding. He said 'oh you are not pursuing M.Pharm in Pharmacology. What a waste of a person you are. Cheeh! You should be thrown in dustbin'! And then he said something in Kannada to the sweeper, which left everyone laughing except me."Recalling that incidence, I started sweating even more profusely.

"Oh my dear! This man is dangerous." Simran was still laughing.

"How can any professor send you to jail for not answering his question in viva and how can he throw you in dustbin for not opting his subject in M.Pharm? He is a crazy creature." I was feeling nervous. I had never felt that much nervous even while facing our Princi. We reached college.

"Simran you wait here. Let me go in and face the carrier of death."

I was more than afraid to enter his cabin. Since first year he was the only teacher whom I feared. I didn't even dare to make eye contact with him. He was nick named as Hitler, but for me his status was above Hitler. I knocked at his door ever so gently. I had never knocked so gently even in hospitals.

"Come in." The moment I heard that voice I felt like running away.

"Good evening Sir. You called me?" I asked as politely as possible.

"Yes Akash. Sit down." I was taken aback. Sir was offering me a seat, that too on a chair, not a stool. It was like Laloo Prasad offering his CM's chair to me.

"No sir. I am okay." I tried to act decent.

"Sit down." I don't know if he shouted or spoke in his normal voice. But I felt that if I didn't sit then he would shout so loudly that all professors from nearby cabins would come running to see who was getting scolded so badly. In a flash I was on the chair.

"How are your studies going on?"

"Fine sir." I gave the shortest reply possible. "Are you regular in your classes these days?"

"Yes sir. I do attend my classes regularly." I was thinking why the hell was I there. Now he would give me a big lecture on studies. Is that why he had called me for, all the way from Santhala?

"You are from Patna, right? I heard this time Lalu has chances of winning again." Heaven's sake! Give me a break. Has he called me to discuss politics? Personally, I believed that people in Bihar have become mature enough not to vote Lalu again to power. But somehow contradicting Mallik Sir, didn't seem to be a viable option.

"Yes Sir. You are right, he is very popular and there is no other leader even close to his stature." All the while I was wondering how come Mallik Sir knows about my hometown. I always thought, only thing he knows about me apart from my name was that I am the bunker number one of this college.

"Cheeh man! How come people are so ignorant to vote constantly for a person who is involved in so many scams?" Mallik Sir said in his same high pitch tone. I was cursing myself why I didn't contradict him. Now he must be thinking that I am one of those ignorant brats. Akash get ready for the blurting. It can come out any moment now. But surprisingly his facial expression was quite calm. May be he is not on his 'Killing mission' now.

"Hey Akash do you still play carom? You used to spend more time playing carom than studying in CL during B.Pharm." Mallik Sir's serious tone made me think that I was wrong. May be he is in his 'Killing mission'. He is just warming up to the occasion. May be he is getting all the info before he could start his blast job. First he enquired about my attendance, and then my political belief and now how I spend or rather waste my time. Akash get ready for a major blasting this time. It's coming. It's bound to come now.

"I used to play a lot of carom in my college days. But these days I play only with my son." Mallik Sir was smiling. Mallik Sir plays and he has a son too! And he can even smile. I could never ever imagine this man out of his lab or taking lectures and horrifying students. The only game I though he plays was to play with his experimental animals. But it seemed he was a human too and of course he was not a Hitler. At least as of now it appeared, that previously I understood him wrongly.

For the next twenty five minutes or so he spoke about all sorts of irrelevant things from cricket to Kashmir, politics to poverty. I was not sure what he was up to, but I must say it helped me know that side of Mallik Sir which I was never aware of. Then he came to the point, "Akash I have heard that you don't want to participate in Utsav. Look my dear when there is interest of college involved, you have to overlook your own personal interest. I am not pressurizing you, but I have seen you act and I think that's the only thing you are good at." There was an extra emphasis on the word 'only'. I was wondering if that was a compliment and if I should say thanks. But if someone says you are good at only one thing, it can't be a compliment. I was confused. So, I just gave a nod. That's the best thing to do, when you don't know what to do.

"I hope I have made myself clear. I think you won't be bunking the cultural events, the same way as you used to bunk my lectures in B.Pharm." Mallik sir was laughing. Goodness gracious, has he cracked a joke!

"Sir you were one of the finest professors in my B.Pharm. I had maximum attendance in your subject only."

I know it was all a lie and nothing else. But I thought a bit of lie was okay, if that can make Mallik Sir a bit more blissful. After all it was the first time when he interacted with me and had not scolded me. I was also trying to make my best effort to make him feel good. "Cheeh man! You think I don't know you used to sleep in my lectures? Akash, don't think that you can hide everything behind your specs." I was dumbstruck! That was the most shocking statement of the century. I always thought that I am smart enough to sleep in lectures without getting noticed. I used to boast a lot about this quality of mine.

"Sir…how you…Sir…why you never…" I was blabbering something. Of course my thoughts were not coming out in the form of proper words.

"Akash, you may leave now." Mallik Sir said in his deep husky voice, but his face was smiling.

I briefed about my encounter with Mr. Killer to Simran while returning to the hostel. I was wondering if I should continue calling him by that name, or that has to be changed now.

"So you mean to say that Mallik sir knows a lot about your personal life?" Simran was also surprised like me.

"Yes. You know Simran I must confess that I have judged this person all wrong. Actually we see our lecturers and professors in classroom and lab just for few hours and we think that's their total personality. We usually forget that they too have a life like us. They also can be fun loving, they also can play sports, they also can watch movies and yes they also can be smart!"

"And don't forget that they were also students once. So they know very well how we guys think." Simran had a point.

"Think Simran, Mallik sir used to notice me sleeping in lectures. But he never insulted me in lectures rather he decided to ignore it. How can I call this person Hitler?" I felt shameful.

"You know one of my Uncles is a lecturer in an Engineering college. He told me once, that they discuss about students among themselves, like we do about our lectures. That student is not necessarily the topper or something like that. He can even be a back bencher for that matter. But there must be something interesting about him. It may even be about his affairs in college." Simran giggled.

"Don't tell me! It's hard to imagine someone like Mallik sir and *Sher khan* discussing about love life of their students. But it's possible. After today's conversation I am sure even they are as human as we are and for normal human beings, love is the matter of discussion of top priority." I too started giggling.

"So it means you are participating in Utsav now?" Simran enquired.

"Simran I am still not sure, but one thing is for sure that I have to rethink now. After all it's the 'Hitler's order.'" We had reached Simran's hostel.

"Ok Akash. See you in the mess. Bye." Simran went inside her hostel and I walked towards mine.

My mobile rang again. It was Shashank, "Sir, where are you?"

"Are you insane? Why did you take the matter of my non participation in Utsav to Mallik sir? You think I can be pressurized like this?" I spoke with unreserved anger.

"Sir I called you to explain all this. I was calling you for last one hour or so. But your mobile was switched off."

"So what should I have done? Entered the cabin of 'Hitler' with my mobile on? So that you can call me to explain the things?" I was in no mood to spare him. "Sir please tell me where are you? Are you in Santhala?" Sanky repeated his previous question.

"I am on my way to hostel."

"Sir, can you please come to canteen. We will have tea and ciggie." Sanky knew very well that I won't deny tea and ciggie.

"Ok I will be there in five minutes."

When I reached the canteen, I saw DP was also sitting there with Sanky. Sanky had arranged for his cover. He knew DP was my favourite junior. Since his 'introduction' days he became my favourite. Introduction is actually a misnomer which is just a friendlier name for ragging. In MCOPS we call it intro, rather than ragging. DP's actual name is Dhananjay Patel, which I found a bit too long and boring. So, I gave him that name, DP. It's customary for seniors to name the juniors with some shortened name during intro time. Like Shashank becomes Sanky, Vikram becomes Vicky, Arvind becomes Amu, Bipin becomes Bips, Prateesh becomes Prat, Simran becomes Sims and so on. Usually these names become more popular than their original names. Fortunately or rather unfortunately I was never nick named by my seniors.

"Come *Bhaiya*. Have a seat." DP addressed me as *Bhaiya*, which he had done right from his first day in the college. Usually I don't like my juniors calling me *Bhaiya*, but DP was an exception. There was some sort of innocence in him. Somehow I liked it when he called *Bhaiya*, so I never stopped him.

Sanky lit the ciggie for me and soon tea also came.

With a puff of ciggie I said to DP, "It's been three years here in Manipal. At least now you start smoking dude."

"Akash *Bhaiya*, I have learnt so many good things from you. Let this one go by."

DP said smiling. I too smiled back.

"Sir you must be thinking that I have deliberately informed Mallik sir that you are not participating in Utsav but it's not like that." Sanky started to speak sensing that my mood is not that bad.

"I went there to discuss the tentative name of participants in all the events. When he saw that your name was nowhere in any of the events, he enquired further. I said that you yourself didn't want to participate, so your name was not on the list. Then he asked me for your number saying that he wanted to talk to you."

If Sanky would have said the same thing an hour before, I would not have believed him but with this new found Mallik Sir I knew that it was very much possible.

"Akash Sir, I knew that you won't like it if Mallik Sir calls you, and you will be mad at me. I even thought of saying that I didn't have your number or something like that. But you know how 'Hitler' is! It's difficult to lie to him. And you know he called you right then in front of me, so I could not even inform you that Mallik Sir might call you." Sanky's voice was very apologetic.

"It's ok *yar*. It's not such a big issue." I smiled. Ciggie and tea always soothes me.

"So it means that you are participating?" Sanky asked with a beaming smile.

"That, I have not yet decided." My state of mind has changed from 'not participating' to 'not decided'. That was all due to Mallik sir.

"*Bhaiya*, I don't care what you decide. But I have decided that you are directing the acting events. I can force you. I have that right. If you consider me as your brother, you will listen to me and if you don't listen, mind you I can forcibly take you also. So, you have to come. You come happily on your own or you come by force, I don't care. It's your brother's wish and you need to fulfill it. That's all." DP spoke everything in one go. No doubt he is a good actor and his dialogue delivery is also excellent. I was wondering if he had rehearsed it before or it was natural? That's the problem with actors like us. When we speak from our heart, people think that we are acting and when we are actually acting, people think that we are genuinely speaking. I looked into DP's eyes and I could sense he was natural. After all I was the director and I could make out the difference between genuine and fake emotions. That was it! I decided. My state of mind had changed from 'not decided' to 'decided'.

"DP, come to my room after 12. We will decide upon the personnel for the acting events." DP like me was a nocturnal animal and we loved to work on scripts and other things during night.

"Oh Sir. I knew you couldn't deny DP." Sanky was now finally relieved.

"So Mr. Cultural secretary may I take your leave now? It's almost dinner time."

Before Sanky could reply DP said, "Go *Bhaiya* go, I know someone is waiting for you at dinner!" I could understand his remark in that line, but I let it go. People who are close to you do have the right to pass comments like this sometimes.

At about 12.15, DP and Sanky came to my room. Sanky was also a heavy smoker like me. The moment he entered the room, we lit our ciggie.

"Akash *Bhaiya* I can't believe my luck. My best friend Sanky and my closest senior are both smokers. God knows how I will survive till morning. It seems I am sitting within two chimneys." DP, who was a non-smoker showed his concern.

"Nothing will happen to you. When nothing happened in three years, nothing will happen in one night for sure. Understood you moron?" Sanky spoke as only close friends do.

"You know very well DP, I can't think anything creatively without smoking. It has become an involuntary action." I smiled. "Now we better start our work."

For the next few hours, we three worked on selecting the right actors for the right events. Some were good at comedy, some were good at emotional scenes, some were good at giving loud expressions, some were good at speaking in loud pitch without getting hitched, some were good at mocking Bollywood actors and actresses while others were good at silent acting. So we selected each one accordingly for each event.

We always tried to make a skit which was emotional with a bit of comedy in between just to add spice. We always kept the ending emotional, rather a sad ending. It always appealed to the judges and the audience if we finish the skit with some high drama emotional scene. That last impact always made judges give us a few extra points. Mimes were mostly comedy as it was much easier and appealing to do a silent comedy rather than a silent emotional scene. Mad ads were always an outright comedy. When the name itself is 'mad' there has to be madness, which can be best created by comedy. So we had to carefully select who could be utilized in which event. In addition, there were some, who were common in all events. Moreover many of our old team members were not in Manipal anymore. So the selection of new members had to be done, which made our task even more difficult. We had seen them act before in various colleges and other events, but even then,the selection was difficult. Finally at about 4 am we had our cast ready.

"Sir, this time also you are adopting the same old

formula or any change?" Sanky asked casually.

"I don't think there is any need to change. It's a super hit formula and why to experiment?" I spoke as if I were a Bollywood director speaking about my forthcoming movie.

"Sanky we all know that if Akash *Bhaiya* dies or cries at the end of the skit, no one can stop us from winning," DP said and then began laughing.

"Hahaha... very true! After Big B and SRK its Akash Sir whose death at the end can guarantee the success." Sanky was still smiling.

"Enough guys. Enough of pulling my legs. Now go to your room and let me sleep. I have to attend morning lectures." I threw the bud of my last ciggie.

"Since when have you started thinking about lectures?" Sanky asked surprisingly. "You don't know, Akash *Bhaiya* has got some motivation now." DP again passed his expert comment.

"One word more and I will kick your ass."

"DP you remember our first Utsav, when we were in the first year and Akash sir was in third year?" I guess Sanky was trying to change the topic.

"Yes I remember very well. How can I forget that? It was my first stage appearance in Manipal. I myself did not know that I was so good at comedy. God knows how Akash *Bhaiya* came to know about it." DP was perplexed.

"It's all because of those intro sessions." I said as a factual senior.

"You know DP, that time I did not know Akash Sir very well. I had heard about him that he is a good actor and all, but had never seen him on stage." Sanky seems to be digging in the past. "I was sitting in the audience to watch the skit. A few guys of Dental college of Bangalore were sitting beside me. The moment our skit started, Akash sir made his appearance on stage as he was the narrator."

"Yes I remember very well. The skit was on 'Homelessness,'" DP said.

"And you know what those Dental guys said when they saw Akash Sir?"

"What?" I asked promptly, as it was new information for me and like any other actor I was also very much interested in knowing the reaction of the audience, that too from a rival college.

"They said, 'oh my god it's the same narrator. Fuck! He was also there last year. At the end he cried like hell, spoke some heavy emotional dialogues and committed suicide. That last scene got these mother fuckers award. If he does the same this time, no way our college is going to win. He is fucking good, this bastard.'" Sanky was smiling.

"We all know he is good. What's the big deal if those teeth cleaning sweepers thought so?" DP was visibly pissed off after hearing all those curse words for me.

"You didn't get my point DP. We all know he is good in MCOPS. But think of a guy who has seen him a year before and never ever heard of him again. If that guy recognizes him the moment he sees him, imagine the kind of impact Akash Sir has left on them. Moreover he outright rejected any chance of winning for his college, if Akash Sir is a part of skit team. That very moment I was sure that Akash Sir is some kind of Bond in acting." Sanky was still smiling.

"Enough *yar*. One or two words more and I will fly off to Bollywood. Then who will participate and win in Utsav?" I was also smiling. DP and Sanky also joined. Soon we said good bye to each other. When I was on my bed I was thinking what Mallik sir had said. He said the 'only' thing I was good at is acting. And now it was reconfirmed after knowing this incidence, which Sanky told. Now I was sure that not only I would participate, but I would win it also for myself, for my college, for my core team, and most importantly for all those who believe in me.

Next day DP and Sanky met me in college. I organized a meeting with all my potential team members and made it clear what I wanted from everyone. I was back to the job, which I do best! All the time I was thinking about scripts, characters and dialogues whether I was watching TV, playing carom, eating food, my mind worked equivocally on just one thing. At night DP used to come to my room and we used to discuss till 4 o'clock in the morning. Occasionally Sanky would also join us. We used to do our rehearsals during college hour in the college auditorium.

There were a few jitters, few mishaps, and few differences of opinion but overall it was shaping up well. We all practiced very hard, tried to give our best. Soon, just fifteen days were left. It meant that colleges would get an opportunity to practice on the main stage. As per the protocol of Utsav, all colleges are allocated their slot for using the main stage. It was kind of a dress rehearsal.

"Sir after three days, on Monday we will have the stage." It was Sanky. "I think we would practice for fashion show at night, dance events at evening, singing in the afternoon and acting events in pre-lunch session. Is that ok with you?" "Ya Sanky, that's fine." So, now the day was approaching.

In the next two days we practiced even harder. I wanted all my three events; skits, mimes and mad ads to be perfect before hitting the main stage on the day of dress rehearsal. It was really tiresome as I was both into acting and directing in all three events, although in mimes I had kept my character very short and it was handled mostly by DP. It was just like preparing for my sessional exams when one didn't get time even for eating and bathing. Only difference was that, I was enjoying it from the core of my heart. Soon it was the night before the dress rehearsal. All my team members were in the college.

"My friends, tomorrow we would get an opportunity to practice on the main stage. I want everyone to think that the stadium is full of audience and you are performing in front of the judges. Even if you commit any mistake or forget anything, don't stop. Once we start, we will stop only after finishing. Improvise promptly if anything goes wrong, but don't let anyone else know that you have done any mistake. Tomorrow is the day! If we guys can do it tomorrow, we will certainly do it on the day of competition also. So, everyone give your best. Today, no night practice. All of you go to your rooms now, sleep well and come tomorrow at sharp 9 am, all geared up!" It was a customary speech, which I always deliver to boost up my team.

That night I could not sleep. I was so excited thinking that I would be on that stage once again. The same stage which gave me name, fame and recognition in Manipal. The same stage which brought Neelu in my life. The same stage where the Vice Chancellor of Manipal, himself praised me. So many memories, so many incidences right from my first year to final year. I was feeling nostalgic. My memory kept going back to that Utsav when I was in third year. I could never forget that pre Utsav night when I was sitting with Neelu on that stage.

UTSAV - Down the memory lane

✻ ✻ ✻

That Utsav was also like any other Utsav,busy, hectic and full of fun. I was two years younger then, so obviously excitement was much more and of course Neelu was also around. So it was the time of double excitement for me. But in spite of Neelu being part of my skit team we hardly could manage to talk to each other. During our practice session we were always crowded by our fellow team members. So there was no scope of any personal talk. Once skit practices were finished, I was occupied in mimes, mad ads whereas Neelu would run for her singing and dancing practice. It meant even our customary 10.30 phone calls were not happening, although Neelu had a mobile then. If I was the undoubted cultural king, Neelu was no less than cultural queen. She was in high demand for choreography of solo and group dance. Even in group song she was mandatory. For some strange unknown reasons she never used to participate in solo singing competition, but she always gave proper guidance to the singers. She was a trained singer after all. In short we both were running here and there from one practice centre to the other till the hostel gate closed. It had been almost fifteen days that I hadn't talked to Neelu even for two minutes in peace. During practice session I used to shout more than talk. I become an animal when it comes to practice sessions. It was the afternoon before the start of Utsav and we were done with our final rehearsal. I deliberately let my other team members go and casually stopped Neelu. We were walking towards her hostel. Although her hostel was not in my way, but I decided I needed to talk to her that day at least for few minutes. We were just discussing Utsav and nothing else.

"Akash this time we will surely win the group dance. It is really coming out good. But I am still doubtful about solo dance. That girl Shweta is real stupid. She always forgets the steps." Neelu was passing on the information.

"Then why don't you yourself participate in solo dance?" I asked her the same question, which I had already asked about fifteen times.

"Akash, you know very well I don't participate in solo events."

"Yes I know. But I still don't know the reason. I am puzzled by your approach." I felt disgusted.

"Everything doesn't have logic or reasoning dear." Neelu said with her charming innocence, which meant that there was no more scope of argument left for me. "Anyway, how about your singing practice? Last time you guys won in group singing, but Punam could not win it in solo."

"Hopefully this time we would win both in group and solo," Neelu said with a glitter in her eyes.

"I hope so. We need to win in both singing and

dancing to beat KMC. In fashion show MIT would win. It's difficult to beat those bastards."

"Akash! Language! There is no need to curse participants of other colleges. Whoever is good will win." Neelu was about to start her philosophy all over again.

"Bull shit. They are our enemies and they are no more than fucking bastards for me." I deliberately used curse words again.

"It's impossible to talk to you guys. Anyway, forget it and don't be too much bothered about my practice of singing and dancing. You better concentrate on your mad ads and mimes, because you don't have Neelu there, the best actress of all times." Neelu flashed her eyelids rapidly and stared laughing. I also joined her. We had already reached her hostel. In fact, for last ten minutes we were standing outside her hostel.

"Akash let me go now. Bye dear."Neelu said and instead of going inside her hostel, she started walking towards the college.

"Hey Neelu, wait! Are you going to college?" I was surprised.

"Yup. I have my dance practice now."

"So, what about your lunch?" I was again surprised.

"Well I had just fifteen minutes time, but I lost that in chit chat with you. So I need to rush now." Neelu was smiling.

"What rubbish is this? If you reach late by fifteen minutes, it won't make a difference." I was feeling a bit guilty.

"How can you say like this Akash? Don't you remember how much you shout when someone is late in your practice?"

"I am sorry Neelu. You will have to remain hungry

because of me." My guilt was now obvious in my words.

"Don't speak like a moron. I was with you by choice, not by compulsion. Come on *yar*, I can bunk one lunch for a close, special one like you.""Ok dear." I was still in my guilt world.

"Now cheer up and let me rush. Bye!" Neelu walked away in the familiar gait of her half walking and half running.

On my way back to my hostel three words were echoing in my ears… 'close, special one'. I was dragged back to the real word when I heard someone calling my name. It was Punam . After the customary 'Hi', 'Hello' I casually asked her, "So, Punam Ma'am which song are you singing in Utsav this time?" I used to call her Ma'am as she was my senior, Neelu's batch mate.

"You are asking as if you don't know!" She made faces in a typical girlish style.

"How will I know Ma'am? Whoever sings the song keeps it a secret, so how would I know?"

"That's true, but if the person who is singing shares every secret with you, then obviously you would know." She was smiling very cunningly.

"What you mean Ma'am?" These girls can make you crazy.

"I mean why don't you ask your loving friend. I am sure if you ask her, she would definitely tell you." That cunning smile was now transformed into a mischievous smile.

"Whom are you talking about?" I was in no mood of solving riddles. "One and only one, your Neelu Darling." Punam Ma'am was looking at me with a shrewd smile. To say that I was surprised would be an understatement.

"Ok Ma'am. See you." I was not in a mood of talking to her anymore and see her making fun and bullying me.

I was wondering such a fool I am! I asked about solo dance, but didn't bother asking about solo song. I just presumed that it would be Punam singing the solo song. And this Neelu! She is also such a...She could have told that she was singing solo, but no, she didn't. That's how she was! But if she was singing solo what was the big deal in that. Why was I getting so restless. I reached my room, lit a ciggie and tried to relax. But I could not. I knew that unless and until I hear the song, which she was going to sing, I wouldn't feel ease. I wouldn't be able to concentrate on any damn thing. But how the hell would I meet her? I mean, I had already met her in the afternoon and we both were so busily packed in Utsav preparation. If I ask her to meet again today, she would surely kill me. But tomorrow is her performance, so I need to meet her by tonight. I decided that there is no point in messing around. Better call her and fix the meeting. As expected there was a blast from her side, "Have you gone crazy? We already met in the afternoon. Then why you want to meet again?"

"Neelu it's something urgent. I can't tell over the phone." I tried to create some suspense just to make my case strong.

"What is this Akash? You are scaring me now. Tell me, what it is?" Neelu was still reluctant to come.

"It's ok, if you don't have time, let it be. I can manage fine." I tried yet another EB. "So, you won't listen. Okay. At 9 pm. But remember just for ten minutes. Not even a minute more." I knew my EB would work.

"Ya Neelu, not even a half minute more. Meet me at the main stage." I smiled and hung up the phone.

Soon it was time to meet my princess. I was busy practicing for mimes in college till then. I reached main stage at 9 pm sharp. As expected there was no sign of Neelu till then. The stage was kind of empty as no practice was allowed a day before the Utsav. There were only a few decoration guys who were giving the final touch. I wondered when Neelu would come, as I had only half an hour time in hand. I was suppose to be at Mimes practice at 9:30 after dinner. I had never been late to any of the practice sessions. If director himself starts coming late, what message would it give to the other members? May be first time I would be late tonight. At 9.10 Neelu came huffing and puffing. Whenever she comes late she will show as if she had come running a 100 meter race in ten second. After all she was a good actor. But I was also a director. I could make out very easily that it was all acting. She held a small packet in her hand. The moment she came near me, she started shouting, "Are you mad? What's the matter? You know if I go late for practice, Punam will take my life for all money."

"Shall I call Punam Ma'am and ask her not to take the life of 'my life'?" I said with a teasing smile and began dialling the number. She snatched my mobile and said, "This stupid mobile is the cause of all problems. If you don't have this, you won't be able to contact me at all. Then at least there would be some peace in my life." She was also smiling. But within a second she was serious, "Tell me fast, why have you called me?"

"Just like that. I was missing your cute smile and pretty face. Just wanted to see that." I again teased her. There was an atom bomb explosion. Neelu lost all her cool. She kept cursing me for five minutes, saying how immature and childish I was, how there should be some limit to my pranks and many more stuff like that.

After her outburst of anger, she became a bit normal and we talked normally for a few minutes. Then I asked very casually, "Neelu which solo song are you singing?"

She said almost promptly, *"Lag ja gale se..."*

Then all of a sudden as if she remembered something, "How the hell did you know that I am singing in solo? It is a secret, only Punam and I know."

"You don't know all the girls of your class reveal all their secrets of heart in front of me very happily. You know I am something special." I tried to give a SRK effect. I guess the actor inside me was taking a toll on me.

"You donkey, have you ever seen your face!" Neelu obviously didn't like my playboy type dialogue. "'The girls of your class reveal all their secrets of heart in front of me very happily.' Neelu mocked my words in a funny accent. "You are a real donkey."

"Ok Neel, whatever. I need to hear that song." I came to the point without messing around anymore.

"Now I know very well why you were dying to meet me. Don't even think of it. I am not going to sing at all. Just hear it on the stage tomorrow." Neelu acted as if she is very annoyed.

I knew it won't be easy to convince her to sing. I requested again and again. That same quarrel, same fight, and that same pampering which is normal between us happened. And in the end I used my master stroke, my EB.

"Neel why you always make me beg before you even for small little happiness? Can't you just listen to me even once?" I was about to say a few more emotional, heavy duty dialogues, but Neelu stopped me in between. "Akash, please stop it. Okay! But I will just sing one para, not the whole song." Neelu again acted as if she is very irritated. I can make out when she is acting.

"Ok Neel, its fine."

Neelu started singing the song. I can't say how I felt at that moment. I was just looking at her even without blinking my eyes. I was about to get lost in her eyes. She sang the first line, "*Lag ja gale, ke fir ye haseen rat ho na ho…*" And then she stopped.

"You donkey, if you keep staring at me like this, I won't be able to sing." This time her voice had a mixture of shyness and irritation, which seems to be genuine. "Oh, is that so? And how do you think you will be singing on stage, when thousands of guys would be looking at you?" I was also a bit irritated.

"I don't care about the thousand guys looking at me. But when you look at me, something happens." Neelu was shying even more now.

If you ask me, I felt that line would have been relevant for a girl who is sixteen and who has fallen in love for the first time. But where Neelu was concerned, unexpected always happens. Nothing is ever normal with this girl.

"Ok Neelu now I would look at the ground, not at you." I just somehow wanted to hear the song. Even I don't know why I was dying to listen to the song. May be I was not normal and behaving like a lover who was just sixteen. Neelu again started singing.

"Lag ja gale, ke fir ye haseen rat ho na

ho...

Shayad phir iss janam me mulakat ho na

ho..."

She stopped again just after singing the first two

lines. I shifted my gaze from the ground to her face. She stared laughing and hid her face in her palms. God! Why is she blushing so much? Do all girls behave like this or Neelu was really a special case.

"Akash, I have one request. Tomorrow please don't come in the singing competition. If I see you, I won't be able to sing," Neelu said in a worried tone this time. I thought she has gone insane.

"I would definitely come and if you don't sing, our college guys would bash you up. So be prepared." I smiled.

"I am telling the truth. If I can't sing when only we two are here, it's definite that on stage if I see you, I won't be able to sing. Please don't come *yar*." Now her voice had a tone of helplessness. I guess my skit practice is showing its effect on me. I am giving too much attention to change in voice tone and emotions.

Time was running fast and there was not much scope of argument, "Ok Neelu we will see what to do tomorrow. But now, please sing the song."

She started singing again. But surprisingly she didn't ask me to look down, neither was she looking down.

"Lag ja gale ke fir yeh haseen rat ho na ho

Shayad phir iss janam me mulakat ho na ho
Paas aaie ki hum nai aaenge bar bar
Bahen gale me dal ke, hum ro le jar jar
Aankhon se phir ye pyar ki barsat ho na ho

Shayad phir iss janam me mulakat ho na ho
Lag ja gale se..."

While singing those last two lines, she was looking directly in my eyes. I hated it when she look this way, because then I started loving her even more. I can never forget those looks. I can never forget those emotions. I can never forget those two drops of pearls in her eyes. There was something in those eyes, which made me feel that this night would never come again, as the lyrics of the song actually meant. I should stop her tonight. Tonight is the day when our love would reach its climax. I should not let her go tonight. No one knows what might happen tomorrow.

"*Tujhe dekha to ye jana sanam*" It was my mobile ringing. My thoughts of romance and love vanished. I knew it would be one of my team mates calling for the practice. I knew I have overshot my dinner break. When I saw the number, it was Punam Ma'am.

"Hello Ma'am."

"Hi Akash. Is Neelu with you?"

"Yes she is with me, but how do you know that?" I was taken aback by that direct question.

"I am trying her mobile for last half an hour. She is not answering. So it's obvious that in such a busy schedule of practice, if she is missing, she has to be with you." Punam Ma'am giggled in a teasing tone.

"Yes, but..." I tried to explain something. "Akash, just tell her that we will be practicing in Anu's room, not in college and time is sharp ten. She knows the time though, only the venue has changed." Punam Mam stressed on timing more than required.

"Ok Ma'am. I will tell her. Bye."

I looked at my watch. Only ten minutes were left to 10 pm. I passed on the information about change in practice venue and timing to Neelu.

"Neelu I guess you have to miss your dinner now.

I am so sorry *yar*. You have to stay hungry for the night just because of my stupidity. Even in the afternoon you didn't have your lunch." I had a genuine guilt in my voice and I guess Neelu realized that.

She started laughing. That same laugh, which drives me crazy.

"You are a real donkey. Don't be so sad! I knew you wouldn't let me go in ten minutes. So I have already made my arrangements for dinner. I have brought Maggi." Neelu showed me the packet she was carrying.

"Within five minutes I would reach room. In two minutes I would prepare it. In another five minutes I would eat up and by 10.10 pm I would be in practice. And in our practice, ten minutes late is allowed. Everyone is not as strict as you Mr. Director." Neelu blinked her eyes.

That last line reminded me that even I am late, that too by half an hour.

"Ok Neelu, you rush. See you later."

"Bye Akash." Neelu almost ran into her hostel.

I also headed towards the practice venue. I could not afford to eat even Maggie for my dinner. I was damn late. For the first time I would be late for my practice session. On my way, I was just thinking about the lyrics of that song and was wondering if this night would ever come again in my life?

Today I have the answer. That was really the last night of our love and romance.

After that, our relationship took a downfall. Neelu was never that same Neelu again. Things became bad to worse. That pre Utsav night remained the last night of my romance and hence I can never forget it.

My chain of thoughts was interrupted by the ringing alarm in mobile. It was 6 in the morning. I rescheduled my alarm to 8 am. I needed to sleep at least for two hours before hitting the stage for the dress rehearsal.

Next three days were my most memorable ever. We bagged the first prize in both skit and mimes. In mad ads we came second. Even in JAM and extempore I came second. Most surprising was getting the first prize in Dumb Charades in which I participated for the first time. We also won in Fashion show, group dance, instrumental, rangoli, mimicry and many other events. It was the best ever performance of MCOPS. We won the overall champions trophy. Those five minutes when we all were on the stage, holding the trophy were the most memorable five minutes of Manipal.

As soon as Utsav was over, it was time for third sessional. In the third sessional,the positions got swapped again between Nishtha and me. She was on second position this time. I did not even realize that one year had just finished, until dates of University exams were displayed. Time really flies in Manipal. I felt as if it was yesterday when my M.Pharm had started. Anyway I again followed my usual exam period routine. But this time the preparatory period was of twenty days, rather than just ten days. Rest all of the things were same. Soon exams were over and we all were awaiting results. It was our last few days in Manipal, as in our second year we had to take industrial project.

Results came within a week. I was first class, distinction holder, and topper of M.Pharm batch. Nishtha also got distinction and so did Simran. I was not surprised or overwhelmed, just happy with my results. After my performances in sessionals and practicals, it was kind of expected. Somehow, being the best in the batch was not as fascinating as it was in the beginning. But even then I felt satisfied as for the first time I could proudly talk about my marks to my parents.

By that time we all had taken up projects in various companies and we all were leaving Manipal within two or three days. Actually we all were waiting for results before reporting to our respective companies.

30th September 2006, Last Night at Manipal

* * *

Manipal life was almost over. I got a project in Lintac Pharma Limited, Bangalore in Product Management Team (PMT) and Simran got project in Jubilant Pharma, Delhi in Intellectual Property Rights (IPR). It was our last dinner in BQ mess.

We loitered around the campus the entire day. We tried to capture the memories of our time spent in Manipal through our eyes. Simran was vocal and chirpy throughout the day, as always.

But as soon as she entered the mess, she fell silent.

"What are you thinking about, Simran?" "Nothing *yar*."

"I know you are thinking about something." "How do you know that?"

"This is the first time in the last one year, that you are listening more than speaking. So obviously you are thinking something." I laughed, thinking that Simran would also join me, but she remained serious.

"Oh Ya! One year! Akash one year is not such a large time span. But I have developed so much liking for this place. And you have become such a nice friend. No one ever understood me the way you did. I will miss you so much." It's very rare that Simran talks any kind of emotional stuff. She usually avoids this kind of an emotional show. The only time I remember her getting emotional was when she had a major fight with Raj. I really didn't know how to react.

"Simran true bonding is not measured by the time spent together or the favour done for each other, but by the comfort you find when you realize that you have each other. And wherever we go, we will be there for each other. So you need not worry and think *yar*, Raj is there in Delhi. You guys will have a rocking time."

"That's true Akash. Raj is the only reason I have opted Delhi for my project. It's been one year since I have seen him. I really want to be with him now."

"Good. Come on now let's go to Saiba. We will have an ice cream one last time."

"Akash, don't keep on repeating 'last time' again and again."

"Ok. Let's be fast. You have your train at 12 midnight. We should reach the station by 11. You have so much of luggage also."

"This Mangala Express has such odd timings. 12 midnight! It's so confusing to book the tickets. The date changes immediately after its arrival.

Simran was once again talking and laughing, which meant she had overcome her emotional outburst.

We reached the station on time. I had come to see her off and helped with her luggage. I had never imagined that I could do any such thing in my life for a girl. But with Simran the case was different. I didn't know how and when it became insignificant that she is a girl. I guess gender becomes immaterial in true friendship. Only thing that mattered was that Simran was a person I really liked. We were waiting for the train. I had the same feeling crossing my heart that I had experienced one year back when I came to the station to see off my B.Pharm friends. I don't know why I am always destined to see people off. I felt low and had a strong urge to smoke.

"Simran you wait here for five minutes. I'll just come."

"Going to smoke, I guess."

"Yup."

"Ok, I am also coming along with you."

"You? Why?" I was not sure why Simran wanted to accompany me. She had mentioned many a times before how she hated my smoking habit.

"I enjoy passive smoking. I like that smell." Simran smiled and winked. God knows what that meant. I asked one of my juniors to take care of the luggage, who had come to see off his friend. We came out of the station. I lit my ciggie and started to speak about the things which I wanted to keep inside me. I guess it was theme lancholy in my mood brought about by the parting away, that made me speak about those things.

"It's my curse that whatever things I really love, never stay in life for much time. Be it friends, girlfriend, cousins or any other damn thing. I am a very poor guy when it comes to relations."

"You are taking the things into a wrong perspective. You may be separated by distance with your near and dear ones, but there is always an undercurrent of bonding which keeps you together." Simran was sounding too serious and was speaking as if she had too much experience in life. Even after one year, I failed to understand her personality. Sometimes she behaved like an eleven-year-old kid and another moment she could behave as mature as my grandmother.

"Yes Simran, I think you are correct. But still there are some people who are not in my life anymore and that hurts a lot." Smoke came out of my nose as I spoke.

"I know very well that this 'some people' is Neelu. I know you still love her and miss her. I still wonder why and how she left you." That was very true. That 'some people', was none other than Neelu. Simran understood me very well.

"You don't know how we broke up?"

"You never told me and I never asked about this torturing incidence."

"It was no doubt painful and torturing. After my break up I literally had sleepless nights for at least a month. I used to keep looking at the revolving fan whole night, waiting for sleep. Ironically,I used to fall asleep only at the stroke of dawn. It was during those depressing times that I smoked grass for the first time."

"Oh no! So that's one more reason for your attendance shortage in the final year." Simran promptly came to that conclusion.

"Yes! You know it was the month of January and I was in my third year. We had just come back to Manipal after our post Utsav vacations." I was again getting lost in my memories, but this time it was the past I never liked to remember. But I wanted to share it with Simran, I don't know why!

That was our first day in Manipal after vacation. I had not met Neelu yet. Just saw her in college sitting in her classroom. But somehow she avoided coming anywhere close to me. During the break she was sitting in the canteen with her batch mates and by chance I also went there with my group. Everyone greeted each other, guys hugged each other, and girls shook hands as we all were meeting after a long vacation. But very cleverly Neelu managed to avoid greeting me. She did not even say a single word to me. I thought she wanted to greet me in a special manner when we were alone. Now I was just waiting to call her. It was 10.30 at night and I called Neelu. I was dying to hear her voice. For the entire one month I had not heard that magical sweet lovely voice.

"Hi Neelu. How are you? It's good that you are in your room. I was desperate to hear your voice. I wish I could meet you now itself." I took a chance. If she said yes, I could run to her hostel in a flash.

"Hi Akash. We met in college today. Why do you want to meet again?" There was no enthusiasm in her voice.

"Met? Do you call that meeting? You didn't even look at me, forget about talking. Come on *yar*, it's been a month! I need to see you. Want to feel your presence with me." I might have continued speaking, but Neelu intervened.

"Akash its new year." Neelu took a pause. I knew the meaning of that pause. I could understand her silence. I could feel that something was wrong.

"I have decided few new year resolutions. But I need your help to stick to those resolutions. I can't do it alone and I know Akash you will help me, no matter what." Neelu's voice seemed to be coming from a planet faraway. My sixth sense asked me to prepare for some volcanic eruption.

"Yes Neel, I will always be there to help you in your cause. Tell me what your resolutions are?"

"Not on phone. We will meet tomorrow evening at 7 in front of LH. Is that okay with you?" "Yes Neelu. That's fine." I cut the call. It was the first time ever that I had disconnected the call. It is always Neelu who hung up the phone first. I liked to hear her goodbye and then that click sound of putting the phone down. I know that's crazy, but as I have always said there is something in these girls which makes guys lose their common sense. But that day I could not wait to listen to her 'bye'.

Next evening, I was in front of LH exactly at 7 pm. Neelu came late, as usual. That was the only usual thing that happened that evening. After that, everything was unusual. After few useless talks, Neelu came to the point.

"You know my elder sister was having an affair."

"Yes you told me about that."

"She told about her affair to our father. He could not take that shock. He had a mild heart attack. I have told you he is so much against these inter caste marriages."

"Yes Neelu, I know." I know what was coming next. I was preparing myself for that thunder storm.

"Akash my parents would never allow inter caste marriage. And I have taken the New Year resolution that I will never hurt my parents, as my sister did. I want to live as an ideal daughter. I want to live a life which my parents want me to live. Akash let me be that daughter of my mom and dad. I can't do justice to any other relationship in my life. Akash, I beg you to let me go away from your life." Neelu looked at me. Her eyes were wet. I had nothing to speak. Thunder had struck and my heart was burnt forever. I managed a plastic smile and said, "Neelu it's okay. I can understand your feeling. It's impossible that you expect something from me and I can't do that for you. You want me to walk away from your life, that's fine. But can we be in touch, just as friends. At least once in a week can I call you?" Somehow I felt that there was still some hope left.

"No Akash. We will not be talking to each other hence forth. We will be like strangers for each other. Even in college we will not talk to each other." Neelu's words were like a knife tearing me apart. Now even my eyes were wet.

"Ok Neelu. As you wish. Let me go now. Bye." I knew if I stood there even for a minute more, I would start crying.

"Akash, you might be feeling that I am a stone hearted person, but believe me in due course of time you will forget me." I don't know if she was trying to console me or what, but those words felt like an arrow. Before leaving I said just one line, "I will never forget you my whole life Neelu."

I returned to the present where Simran was standing in front of me.

Simran spoke for the first time since I started talking about my break up, "It means it was not totally Neelu's fault. She was also to an extent, helpless."

"Ya, I never blamed her for anything. It was just the case of wrong timing and wrong people meeting under wrong circumstances."

"Hmm." Simran was not sure what to say. "But Simran that last line of Neelu's, that I will forget her in due course of time, hurt a lot. She failed to understand the intensity of my love and I decided that I would show her that I will never ever forget her." "But how will you let her know that you still love her, that you have not forgotten her?" Simran looked worried.

"I have already done that."

"What? How?" Now she was surprised, rather than

worried.

"You see these burn marks on the back of my left palm?"

"Yes, I have seen these many times. These three small round marks. I thought they' there since your childhood."

"No Simran. These I had made deliberately by burning my skin with the cigarette three times." I tried to be calm but my voice was trembling.

"Are you insane? What are you saying?" Even Simran's voice was shaking.

"These marks will be there till my death and till my death these marks would never allow me to forget Neelu. That's the only way I could have proved to Neelu that I will not forget her in due course of time."

"Oh Akash now I know why you got that tag of Love *Guru*. Now I know..." Simran was about to say something, but I stopped her.

"Let it be *yar*. No point in discussing what has already happened. And I think we should go inside the station now. It's almost 12."

Soon train arrived and Simran was gone. The last line she said was, "Akash it's been wonderful in Manipal and you made it even more wonderful."

On my way back to hostel I was thinking about the painstaking work of packing my luggage. In the morning I had to catch the bus for Bangalore and Simran was not here to wake me up. Now once again I was on my own. That's life, people meet, spend time with each other, develop relationships and then part away just to make a yet another new relationship. My college life had finished and I was about to enter my professional life. I was about to leave the place where I had started as an immature teenager who had now transformed into a grown up sensible mature man. I owe so much to this place, which made me the person that I am today.

New Life

* * *

Next morning I was in Bangalore. Two of my batchmates, Prateesh and Saikat were already in Bangalore as they too got their projects in Bangalore. Prateesh was in fact in my company, but in another department. Saikat and Prateesh had already rented a flat, which was near our office. Our flat was a small one but enough for three bachelors. It had two rooms, one kitchen and one bathroom.

After my B.Pharm, it was the first time that I was sharing room with someone and that too with guys who were not very good friends of mine. But with my stipend of just 5k I could not afford a single room. Moreover I was completely a new commodity in Bangalore. So I thought it would be better to have companions. It's amazing how you start thinking rationally, once you are out of college and on your own.

That day, the three of us spent time in turning our flat into a space fit for human habitation. We bought three cots and put them on the floor which would serve as our bed. We tied a rope where we would hang our clothes, obviously we didn't have any almirah, neither there were any wardrobes. We placed a mirror in the kitchen, which was required for our shaving purpose. Obviously kitchen was of no use for us as none of us knew cooking. The only expensive thing we all had were our laptops.

Next morning, I got up at 7 o'clock, that too with just one ring of alarm! That's what sense of responsibility can do to you. It was not a college convocation where I could be late or bunk. It was my first day at office. And with two more guys sharing the same bathroom, and commode I needed to get up early. Since ages I had not taken bath in the morning, but that day was special. I was ready by 8 o'clock; although office timing was 9.30.

Soon Prateesh and I were in office. I felt nervous. There were thousands of things running in my mind. How would my boss be? How would my colleagues be? Would I have to work overtime on the first day itself? Will they give me any time for acclimatization? Do they expect me to give results from day one? And most importantly how would I sit glued to the chair continuously for hours? Knowing my nature, I would be bored pretty soon. I was sure about only one thing, that I would not back off and I would give it my best shot. I would be more serious this time around. I won't be that ignorant brat as I was in my B.Pharm.

About the Author

* * *

Anand was born on August 16, 1980, in Patna. He now lives in Mumbai, with his wife. Post Graduated from Manipal College of Pharmaceutical Sciences (Manipal University) in 2007, he got married in 2013. He is a marketing professional and has worked for various Pharmaceutical companies like Macleod's Pharmaceuticals, Pharmed Limited, Aurobindo Pharma etc. Currently he is working as Therapy Manager with Innovcare Life Sciences. Despite being a hardcore marketing professional for the last ten years, he invests his lone time reading (literature, history and motivational books) and writing (poetry and novels). He is a die hard fan of cricket and seldom misses a live match on TV.

"A Twisted Tale" is the first fiction novel by Anand Kumar, who has captured the essence of a student's college life in his book. The protagonist, after completing his undergrad education, decides to pursue a post-grad degree from the same college. However, the transition is not as easy as he had assumed. The place which he enjoyed to the core during his undergrad years, becomes agonising for him later. He is no longer the same person, neither is his approach. Things change again when he finds someone special. No, not a girlfriend. Flip through the pages of 'A Twisted tale' to unravel the twists and secrets behind the topsy-turvy life of this college go-er.